I0456454

Shiloh

MORGAN'S LEAP BOOK 6

KATHI S. BARTON

This is a work of fiction. Names, characters, places, and incidents are products of the author's imagination or are used fictitiously and are not to be construed as real. Any resemblance to actual events, locations, organizations, or persons, living or dead, is entirely coincidental.

World Castle Publishing, LLC
Pensacola, Florida

Copyright © 2023 Kathi S. Barton
Hardback ISBN: 9798891260870
Paperback ISBN: 9798891260887
eBook ISBN: 9798891260894
First Edition World Castle Publishing, LLC, October 23, 2023
http://www.worldcastlepublishing.com

Licensing Notes
All rights reserved. No part of this book may be used or reproduced in any manner whatsoever without written permission, except in the case of brief quotations embodied in articles and reviews.
Cover: Karen Fuller
Editor: Karen Fuller

The Beginning

Morgan made herself into a tight ball as she hid herself in the tall grasses in the field. She knew that the men chasing her would find her soon enough. But for now, she was going to make them work for it. Never one to give up easily, she knew that this might be her only chance of living. Closing her eyes, trying her best to calm her breathing so that no one would hear it, she did the only thing she knew to do to not think about what was going on around her. Morgan counted to fifty in all the languages that she knew.

She had awakened out here. All she remembered was having dinner in the kitchen with the staff and then waking out in the middle of the moonless night in the part of the yard that the gardener didn't care for very well. To her way of thinking, that was the only reason that the men around her hadn't found her as yet.

Morgan didn't remember going to bed after supper. Not putting on her night gown she had on now. Nor did she remember waking when brought out here in the cool night. She'd been drugged, she figured, and that upset her more than the dirt on her cotton nightgown.

Soon after waking, she heard the voices of the men, six she thought she'd counted, saying that the first one that found her could have her. At fourteen, Morgan knew exactly what that meant. They were going to rape her. Then, more than likely, kill her. Even for as young as she was, she knew that being raped would just about do her in, especially with the six of them wanting her.

Her parents would be looking for her, she hoped. She would admit, only to herself, that they'd not be too upset about her being gone. Neither of her parents were very emotional about her. Thinking that the more she was gone out of the house, the more they liked it. Morgan had a habit of getting up in the middle of the night. To see to one creature or another that had called out to her for one thing or another. So it might be days before anyone—

The hot breath of air on her forehead made

her whimper just a little. Lifting her head without opening her eyes, she felt it once again. It was hot but not sour-smelling. Opening her eyes, she looked right into the golden eyes of a leopard. Their noses touched. That was how close she was to her.

The lick to her face scared her. While she'd seen the wild animals around the compound where she lived, she'd never been this close to one so dangerous. The farmers would kill them when they would take down a cow or something that they raised, but no one could have prepared her for the beauty of them this close. And she was a beautiful cat.

The big cat put her paw on her head and pushed it back down so that it rested on the dirt. When she started to lift it again, the cat pushed her down again. Morgan closed her eyes, understanding that she was to stay where she was. If she was going to be eaten, she was glad that the cat was sparing her from knowing when it was coming.

The sound, soft as a coin dropping onto the dusty ground, was all she heard before the large cat screamed. There was gunfire, too. Something frighteningly close stirred up some of the dirt she was hiding by. The screaming of men was next. She could tell from her hiding place in the weeds that several of them had been screaming. It wasn't long before it was all cut off, and she knew on some level that the cat had killed the men. The paw to her head again had her lifting it up to see if she was next.

The cat had been hurt. Blood was pouring from her shoulder at an alarming rate. Sitting up, unmindful of whether it was safe to do so, Morgan tore at her nightgown to stanch the blood as she spoke to the leopard.

"I think you saved me." The cat just let her poke around at her wound, soon lying down when she asked her to do so. "The bullet needs to come out. If it doesn't, I'm afraid that you'll get sick and die from it. I wish I had my knife here. But I think I can see it enough to get it out with my fingers. I won't do any more than I have to. All right?"

Morgan worked for fifteen minutes to get the bullet out. The cat never hurt her. Never tried to get away from her as she worked either. Sweat poured off of Morgan's forehead as she finally got it free. When she was finished, she showed it to the cat.

"See? Someone got a shot in. I promise you I'll make sure that you're all right and that any sickness that might be on it won't hurt you. Do you have a lair? Someplace that you can rest?" The cat stood up, and that was when she noticed that she'd had kittens recently. "Oh no. Where are they? You left your den to come to save me? Come on. I'll help you back."

It wasn't far. About a hundred yards from where the cat had come to her. It occurred to her that the cat was more than likely saving her kittens from being found when she killed the men, but Morgan was ever so grateful that she'd spared her as well. Helping the cat into the den, she saw that she had three of the puggiest little kittens she'd ever seen.

"They're beautiful. Oh, look at them. You are a good momma, Golden Eyes. They're very fat. I'll stay with you until you need to eat again. Then I'll hunt for you." The cat didn't seem to mind when she picked one of them up, so she touched each of them in turn. "You're very lucky those men didn't find you too. But I guess you knew that." She watched as the fat little cats gathered up around each other for their warmth. "I wish I had a brother or sister that I could cuddle up to. I don't know that they'd like that, but I sure would."

She stayed with the family overnight. There wasn't any way that she'd be able to make her way back home in the darkness, so it was fine with her to be in the cave for the night. The kittens woke hungry a couple of times during her stay there. Instead of having Golden go to them, Morgan carried them back and forth to their mother. She seemed to be all right with her helping that way as well.

When the sun was coming up, Morgan made sure that not only did the family have water, but she also scavenged as much as she could from the horses that the men had come out here in. There was hard tack that was in abundance, but she was also able to get herself some much-needed flint as well as some blankets.

Taking all the things to the cave, she put the kittens on one of the blankets and then sat down to watch them fall over each other until they had their spot picked out. It was calming to watch them, she thought. They were just too little to do much more than be rolly Polly little kittens. She knew too that in no time, they'd be vicious cats that would kill to have a meal. But she didn't let herself think of that right now.

Giving the hardtack to Golden, she made her way to her home alone. It occurred to her how far she'd been carried. Her home was further than she'd thought it might have been, and she didn't arrive there until the sun was nearly down. Going into the house by way of climbing up the back stairs, she heard her parents speaking out their balcony from her own window. Sliding out onto her own, she stood deeply in the shadows to listen to what they might be saying. Her mother was standing at the railing, her father deeper in the room.

"I cannot believe that she's gone." Morgan started forward, wanting to assure her mother that she hadn't been hurt at all. "This was a brilliant idea that you had, Malcomb. To have it look as if she'd been kidnapped and then killed. I have never wanted anything more than that child dead."

Her heart hurt. Her mind didn't know how this was really what her mother was saying, but on some level, she knew that they had always felt like that toward her. They weren't close, but she never thought that she'd want her dead. But even as her dad came out to the balcony, too, she watched the two of them as they stood there in an embrace. Nothing in her mind or heart could have prepared her for what they said about her. Morgan just watched them as tears, hot ones, rolled down her cheeks onto her dirty gown.

"Well, it wasn't nearly as hard as I thought it would be to get some men gathered up to take her. As you said, it's a good thing now that she's gone. When they find her body, it will be blamed on anything but me. I even made sure that they took her out the back way so that the staff wouldn't see them. If you ask me, they've coddled her too much over the years." Mother said that it wouldn't be her fault either. "No. No one will bother with blaming you, my dear. For all they know, you've committed suicide because your daughter is gone. It hurt you to no end that when you went to check on our precious daughter, that her bed was emptied, and her window was opened to the night."

It took her less time than it apparently did her mother for what her father was saying. As soon as he pushed her mother nearly over the railing, intending she was sure to make it look as if she had fallen to her death by her own hand, Mother grabbed her father's coat. The two of them looked as if they'd been out that night.

The two of them hung there for what seemed like forever. Would they both fall? Would they be able to save one another? She didn't care. So when her mother weight, always just enough overweight that she looked plump, it took them both over the edge. Morgan stood there for several minutes thinking about what had just befallen her family. Looking over the edge of her own balcony, she saw them there by the moonlight, tightly embraced as if in a lover's hug and dead. Blood spread out beneath their heads as if a bucket of it had been poured over the two of them. Slipping back into her room, careful of not falling herself, Morgan thought about what she'd just witnessed. The death of the entirety of her family.

Making her way to the kitchen area, she staggered twice in her grief. Not that they were dead, no, it was that they had planned her demise in such a cold way, and it was them that had ended up being dead. Lincoln was there, the butler of the house, when she entered. He took one look at her and sat her in the chair she'd spent more time in than the ones in the formal dining room. Lincoln, along with the rest of the staff that wanted to stay, she knew they would be her family from now on.

"Child, what is it?" She must have been a mess. Or looked on edge. The slap to her cheek stung enough that she was brought out of whatever thoughts she'd been having. "What's happened? Your parents, they told the household that you'd been kidnapped. Are you hurt?"

She told him everything. Not leaving out anything, including the cat that had saved her. Also, leaving no doubt to the older man that her parents had planned for her to be killed this night. Lincoln sat down across from her after making her a cup of tea that was mostly bourbon.

"You are mistress of the house now. Tomorrow, we will find their bodies whilst you are still abed. You will say that you were out with the creatures of the field. They will believe that well enough. That is where you are most of the time." She asked him about the cats. "'Tis your decision. However, if you were to bring them here, none of the rest of the staff will mind. It is you who we stayed for all these years and not your parents. And the only reason that any of us look forward to the day coming to work."

"I'll need help bringing them here." He said that he'd go with her. "They're far. Much further than I had thought. But I wish them to be safe, Lincoln. She saved my life, and I will do the same for her and her family."

"You have a good heart, child. A very good one. We shall leave now and take lanterns with us. A basket, too, so that we might carry the little beasts." She asked him if he didn't want them here. "Nay,

I want what you want. We all do. Tomorrow, after your parents are found, we'll be as we should have been. A good home and a safe one. Also, a home with more love than hate, as it has been for years. Mark my words on that. I will talk to you as we go about now that you are mistress of the house what men will do to get to you. They'll want you, but you're too stubborn to be a good wife to anyone seeking your hand. It might be well that there are cats here to protect you. You have become a very wealthy woman with the death of your parents."

As they were making their way to the cave, she wondered if he knew how safe the house would be with leopards in it. Once the kittens grew up, they'd be as big as she was now. Smiling, she thought perhaps she wasn't all that upset that her parents were dead. They'd been treating her as if she had for as long as she could remember.

Golden seemed happy to see her. She licked her face and brushed her with her large paws. As Lincoln gathered up the kittens, she helped Golden outside to do her business. It took a great deal out of her, and Morgan had to carry her back into the cave. Once they were all loaded up in the buggy, she sat down with Golden to tell her what had happened.

"So I'm motherless except for you. I know that you're a cat and I'm only a human, but I think we can get along. When the men start to come, and according to Lincoln, they will, I'll need you to protect me, too. I shant ever marry. Not only that, but I'm also going to make it my life's work to make sure that animals such as yourself are as safe as I can make them. And you, my dearest friend, will have the best of care that I can give you and the best place in the house."

Arriving home well after the sun had settled in the sky again, she made sure that the mother and kittens were safe in her parent's big bed. There was a fire in the fireplace for them should the night turn too cold. Morgan also made sure too that the mother had plenty to eat, having giving her one of the steaks that her father would treat himself to daily while she had whatever else he had with his meal.

Sleep didn't take it's time capturing by luring her to a night's rest. It hit her right between the eyes and had her nearly sick with exhaustion. As she closed her eyes, sleeping in her own bed as if nothing had happened, she knew that she'd keep her promises to not just Lincoln and the other staff but to herself as well. The animals here would need her, and she was going to make sure that they were as safe as they could be while she was still living.

Four years later

Morgan watched the man as he ran out of her home. How he'd gotten into her home was beyond her, but now that he was gone with a little less of his fancy clothing, she sat down on the front veranda and waited for the cats to come to her. Over the last month or so, men had been showing up at the oddest times to tell her that she must marry them.

They would all come around sooner rather than later, she'd been told. All of her leopards, as well as a plethora of other such creatures, would come to make sure that she'd not been harmed or taken away from them. None of them would be harmed here, she vowed to them all, and daily, another one or two would come limping into the compound and be welcomed. Golden came to sit at her feet, and she smiled at her when she looked at her.

"He had it coming. We both know that. The pompous ass thought that if he could tear at my clothing that I'd allow him to marry me so that I'd be happy. He said that I'd need someone like him to watch over my money and keep me from dying an old spinster. Apparently, women aren't meant to think beyond having a man around." She laughed as she petted her cat while she purred. "I'm much happier without him, I think. What did he think I'd been doing here all alone since my parents were dead? Waiting on someone to recuse me? Not likely." Morgan slid to the floor and put Golden's head on her lap. Running her hand down the length of the cat, she could feel her newest litter wiggling around. "I am worried about you, mistress cat. You're heavier this time with your brood. Not to mention, I know that the wound you suffered for me so long ago bothers you more daily. The babes that you brought here that night they have gone on to have their own children. I cannot believe that so much time has passed since that night." She thought of something and put her forehead to Golden's. "I just realized that you're a grandmother. Congratulations."

"That would make you an Aunt in her eyes." Morgan reached for her gun, something she'd been carrying since that night, and found it gone. "You cannot kill me, mistress, but I would prefer that you not harm me either. I have come to speak with you about the good work you are doing here. The one you call Golden; she has asked me to come to speak to you about a great many things. In addition, I have some things I need to ask of you too."

"Who are you?" The beautiful woman asked if she could tell her in a moment. "So long as you know that whatever it is you're hawking, I want no part of. I'm not going to meet your brother, father, or uncle and marry them simply because someone has it in their head that I need someone. I don't need a man in my life. We're doing very well here on our own."

"You are doing better than well, I think. The ground is fertile here, thanks to your way of doing things. Not all humans would leave an animal to rot on their land without doing something with it." Morgan told her that other animals took care of it. "They have indeed. Even the things that the larger breeds cannot eat or use, the smaller creatures come to salvage what they can. You have a good system here. A system that will not be something popular for a great many years."

"We all make it work because I don't want to have to go into town." The woman nodded, her smile something that she thought was more than beautiful. "You said that you came here because of Golden. She is a cat, a leopard. How is that possible that she would call to you?"

"Let me start at the beginning, please. The

night that your parents died, the night that you came to help Golden, it was thought that you should have died along with them. I'm glad that you didn't, as it turns out, but the earth knows all that goes on. Sometimes, with humans, the apple does not fall far from the tree, and we wrongly assumed you'd be like them. But you are nothing at all like them, are you, sweet child? You were not only different than them, but a kinder, gentler person than any of us have ever seen before. We have all been watching you these last years." Morgan asked her who the *they* were. "Ah, that brings me to your first question. I am Tellus, the terrestrial being that cares for and is wholly a part of the earth. The earth and the land that you have here are only a small part of the earth. Not for my doing but your own. This land is rich beyond anything man has ever seen before."

Morgan didn't speak, letting all that the woman told her to settle into her mind. She'd been alone for most of her life now and had learned not to prattle on when there was no one to talk back to her. Petting Golden, she was glad to hear her purring. The rumbling of her throat was soothing to her for some reason.

"Mother earth. I've read about you. You're

Roman, or at least your name is." She said that was correct. "All right. So you're here because I have good land. However, I still don't know why you took time out of your what I'm sure is a busy day to tell me that. I'm not trying to be rude here, but I know that our lands are rich. It's here to keep me as well as the other creatures that roam here well."

"You are a jewel among all the stars in the sky, Morgan." Confused at the words and their meaning, Morgan continued to pet her cat. "We, the other earth creatures, have been watching what you were doing here since the night of your parents, though it's doubtful that they were any good at that job, had died. We've not had to once intervene in helping you care for the animals, all that you protect here. You have lifted a great burden from all of us. Even creatures that you may not be yet aware of have found a home here among the others and have been safe from harm. One such creature sits there on your leg. His name is Button."

Morgan looked down at her leg and saw the tiny creature standing there. She put out her free hand, and when he hopped upon it, she brought him closer to her face. Yes, he was a little man. Just like the men that had been coming around but for his size. All shiny and dressed up with buckle shoes, too. Then, while she was watching him closely, he spread out his wings and fluttered above her palm for several seconds before settling down again. Nope, none of the others had had wings.

"Faerie." He bowed before her. "I have read of such creatures as this one. My library is full of books about such creatures. They are thought to be a myth. Such as you are, Lady Earth. I have either hit my head, or I'm being visited by creatures that are as magical as the sun coming up and then resting in the other sky."

"You are seeing magic, my child." Nodding, she laid her hand back on her leg. Button didn't sit on her leg again but stayed on her palm. "He wishes to be with you. To help you in the coming years. For as much as I'd like to say your life will be filled with only riches, we both know that it is never that way."

"Nay, it is not. The banker in town says that I owe him great funds for a loan that my parents took out before they died. However, if I were to marry his son, a very lazy man, he would graciously wipe it off his books. My parents have been gone so long ago that I forget their faces now. Also, I have a man who is trying his best to catch me unawares so that he might rape me to take my lands. I don't think he means to keep me around much longer than it is for me to say, 'I do.' They only want what I have, and damn the way that I feel about it." Tellus said that she could help her with those things. "Thank you, my lady. But I'm sure you have enough to do now with the earth as large as it is."

"I do. But helping you is not something that I take lightly, my child. We all, all the creatures in charge of the parts of the earth you now own, are happy to help you. And in doing so, they will get the help they need as well." Morgan asked her what they wanted her to do. "You will do it, will you not. Even not knowing what it is that we ask of you."

"I will help the earth for as much as it gives back to us here. And that, as you know, is a great deal. We are self-sufficient here. Water is ours to use as we see fit. We keep it clean and free of the things that others drop into it like it's nothing more than a trash heap for them. There is a roof over our heads when necessary. The fields, as you have pointed out, are rich and give us back so much more than we can eat. I share what I cannot have put up or preserved." Tellus told her that she knew that as well. "If you need for me to do more, I will do it to the best of my ability."

"Thank you." Tellus looked at her, then at Golden as she continued. "Golden will stay with you until the kittens turn a year old. She will care for them as cats, to show them the way of their kind. You will teach them as well. As only a person such as yourself can do. Her children will be the first of many creatures that will take on this new magic that we wish you to help with."

"She's going to die." Tellus nodded but didn't look at her. "I thought when I've seen her around this time, she wouldn't make it for long after. You do know that she's the only friend that I have besides the people that work here? I've thought about long hours of thinking how I will make it without her counsel. Even though we have never spoken words together, I know her well enough as I do my own mind. Without her snuggling up to me when I need it? Well, I don't know what I would do. But I must, for the others."

"Yes, you will." Tellus told her of the magic that would be given to her. About the babes that Golden would have and how they would go on to be great men. To help her in ways that Tellus and the others hadn't thought of yet. "The magic they will get will help them to be a part of the world of men. To breach such places that, even now, frightens us a little. And as the years and decades go on, it will only get harder for us to navigate. We will need you to help them blend into such places. To walk, talk, and to act like real men. The abilities that we will give to them will make them a prize should anyone find out. So it is important that they do not give themselves away while men. Do you understand?"

"Yes. I'm to be their teacher. You can bet too that they'll be nothing like the men that come around here, my lady." Tellus thanked her and told her, too, that she would be their mother. "I have questions now, but I know I will have so many more when the time comes. I will teach them everything that I can. Give them whatever step up they'll need so long as I live. I promise you they will be the best of men, too. Not like the ones, as I said, that come here sniffing out an easy way to my home."

"You will not die either, Morgan. You will be around for their children to come into the world, as well as all the shifters that are to be born." Morgan asked her about the men coming around that try and get to her. "They will not come around again should you not wish it. Button will have for himself to use an army of faeries that will come to your aid in that and anything else you might need them for. Do not be fearful of using them either, Morgan. Rightly so, they are excited to serve one such as yourself. You have been titled with the name Queen of Shifters."

"You don't have to do that, my lady. I said that I would help you." Tellus laughed, and it made Morgan smile. "I will do as asked. The rest, I will accept it as part of my duties, but I don't see myself using it overly much."

"I foresee you using the magic given to you much more than you think you will. And I'm happy for it." Tellus laughed again, bringing yet another smile to her face. "I will also give you a list of things that you will need to invest in. Things that will be in the future, items and things that will start out slowly but will be a good thing for the world as a whole. These things will fund you better than a bank will, and you will remain self-reliant at the same time. Also, the bank has been taken care of. He will no longer bother you about funds he has lied about that you owe him."

"Thank you for that." Morgan looked down at her friend and ally in all this. "What will become of me when you no longer have a use for me, my lady?"

"There will always be a use for you, child. A creature such as you will forever bond with the earth and make everything around you a better place. I have such faith in you." Morgan told her that she could only do her best. "And that, my child, is all that I could ask for."

The two of them talked throughout the morning and into the evening. Ending up in the living room where there was a fire roaring in the hearth, they were served their tea there as well as juice, too. Morgan was told, too, that she'd need to be drinking a great deal more of the elixir. And the other faeries would make it be abundant for her and the babes to use. She was told that the fresher it was, the better it would be for her after using magic.

At some point, Tellus took her hand into hers and gave her the magic she'd need. The power of it washed over her in waves. So much so that for several minutes, she had to sit still in her seat and wait for it to settle out. Not only did she receive the magic, but the knowledge of how to use it. Also, the list, as she'd been told that she must invest in. Things that Tellus told her that would be worth a great deal in the future. Because no matter how self-reliant she was, there was always a need for money. Taxes were only one of the things that she would need money for.

After Tellus left her to rest, she was told, Morgan sat in the yard at the back of her house. Lincoln, her family butler, and her dearest friend came to sit with her a spell, telling her that there were faeries in the kitchen now that would make sure that the household was safe. Also, he said, he'd been given magic as well.

"It is to keep the house in order. To build this home out when you need it and to keep it in good repair, my lady. And I was told that you would need that in the future." She said that she'd been told she'd need to have a larger house. "I find that hard to believe, but I will do what it takes to have you safe."

"I now have more land as well. Tellus told me that there are now five thousand acres here that will be used for the animals in need as well as us that live here. No one will be able to enter the land if they wish to harm anything that calls this place home. What am I to do with all this knowledge and wealth, Lincoln? I know I'm to teach the next generation of cats born to Golden, but how much do you think they'll need from me? What am I to do when they go out and have their own leap? I shall be an old woman with only you to keep me company." He asked her if he was immortal as well. "You are. But I was told that at any time you wished to die, I could take it from you. No harm will come to you with it either."

"I think I shall stay with you, my lady. I think we will need each other in the coming years, don't you think?" She said that she needed him every day. "You are so kind to me, Morgan, that I wonder at times why your parents wanted you dead. Or, for that matter, if you were actually a child of theirs. You couldn't be more different than they are."

"They were in love with themselves." She knew that to be true as soon as she said it. Looking at the older man, she smiled at him. "You and I will do the best we can and hope that it's right. Someday, I think we'll look back on this and wonder what all the fuss was about. Don't you?"

"I think I will hold my thoughts on that until such time as it comes to an end." He laughed a little. "Do you believe it will come to an end, my lady?"

"No. I don't. I don't have any idea why, but I think we're going to be having something new and something strange happening as a daily routine." She stood up when he did. "Let us begin this new phase of our life, Lincoln, and hope we make it work better than the thoughts in my head are making it. All right?"

"Whatever you wish, my lady. We will do well together, I believe." She hoped so. It seemed like a great deal was depending on her doing just that. Making it work for the safety of all involved. She only hoped that she knew enough and was strong enough to make it work for all of them.

Chapter 1

Shiloh loved the sunny days that were just cold enough to have him needing a light blanket at night and then something light like a sweater during the day. Not that he had one today, but he was enjoying the slightly chilly day. When a shadow fell over him, he opened one eye and looked up. Not believing what he was seeing, he opened the other eye and stared at Rocky.

"I came out here to show you a few markings on my body that you might have as well. It's important that we make sure that we're marked alike so that—what are you doing?" Shiloh said she was naked. "I know that dumbass. How else am I supposed to show you some markings if I'm fully clothed? What are you staring at?"

"You. You're naked." She told him to grow up. "I'm reasonably sure that I'm a grown man. The hardon that I have is killing me right now. A child, hopefully, wouldn't be in this much pain. Why are you naked again? You might have said, but all I heard was 'she's naked' over and over in my mind." She glared at him.

"I need to show you these markings." He nodded, still not sure what she was saying. "You're not going to get anything I'm saying to you right now, are you? Simply because I'm not wearing anything."

"More than likely not. You're very beautiful. While I can understand the need for me to know some of the markings that you have, right now, all I can think about is the fact that you're completely naked. And standing in front of me." She told him that she wasn't in the mood. "Far be it from me to make you think you need to be in the mood for whatever you're...you know what? I'm not even making sense to myself right now. All the blood that was in my head is now in the other one. And it's not thinking well at all. Okay. So you need to show me these markings. Why is that?"

"If we have sex, will you pay attention to me then?" Shiloh told her that if they had sex right now, he'd be a dead man. "Why? You think that I'd kill you or something?"

"No. I'd be doing that all on my own. Trying to keep up with…could you at least put something on? I don't know, something thick and heavy, so I don't see how lovely you are?" Rocky asked him if he really thought she was lovely. "As beautiful as anything I've ever encountered in all my lifetimes."

When she sat on the edge of his lounger, she was dressed. Shiloh wasn't sure if he was glad for that or not, but at least he could focus on the words coming out of her mouth now. And it was a very pretty mouth. When he felt the sting of her slapping him, all he could do was grin at her.

"You're a loon." He thanked her. "That wasn't meant as a complement. It's just my body. Why does it have you all worked up? I mean, in all your years on this earth, surely you've had sex before. Right?"

"Never with you. And never anyone else either so long as we live." He pulled her hand into his and held it. "All right. I'm semi-calmer now. Tell me about these markings. And so you're aware, I have noticed that I have a few marks that I didn't have before. Like the one in the middle of my thigh."

"Yes. That's the one that I need to talk to you about. It's a mark of age. I'm not sure why it's called that. It has nothing to do with age. When I was younger, I would guess about the time you were being created. I encountered a being that I hadn't before. Whenever I meet a new being—not so much anymore—I'm marked as if I were a friend or foe to them. You'll get the same markings now. My memories are now yours. And vise versa. Anyway, the being from the hospital, it was an ancient vampire, he's the one that I met long ago, like I was telling you. But not the kind of vampire that you see today. I've encountered him before, as I said. This one was evil. As most of the vamps now aren't. They've, well, I guess you could say that they mellowed out. This guy, Brad, hadn't. He'd been sent to kill me. Actually, he was to kill you so that he could control me. Which is just stupid because I can't be killed. You can't either now." Shiloh asked why she was to be killed. "That's the question that I've been asking myself for a while now. I'm not doing anything different than I was, say, about a thousand years ago, but here of late, I've been tagged, I guess you could say, in bad beings coming after me. Once, a long time ago, I was a warrior faerie, but I've since given that job up. Well, not so much given it up as I've been fired. Tellus fired me for plotting—I didn't, by the way—to take over her kingdom and rule the earth. I've no more desire to do that than I do a lot of things that I get accused of. Like ruling the earth. Who would want that job? Not me, that's for sure."

"Why not?" Rocky asked him what he meant. "Ruling the earth. Wouldn't that be something that would have a lot of perks? Like, I don't know, ruling people around and shit like that?"

"You've never thought about what it would take to rule the earth, have you?" He grinned at her. "Charmer, aren't you? But to rule the earth, you'd have to be everywhere at once. I don't mean that figuratively, but literally everywhere. Not only would you need to know what is going on at every second of every day, but you'd have to have your hand in all kinds of shit, too, like the other under lords, kings, and queens of the earth broken down so that it's not such a large area to rule in your absences. Then there are the people that work and report directly to you. As a warrior, I never had to do that. I suppose I did, but I never did it. When there was trouble, I went and took care of it. When things were relaxed, I made sure that there wasn't an uprising about to happen. People, beings, can be really stupid when they think of taking over shit that they have no knowledge of. That's why things get fucked up when new management comes in. They think that the job is going to be easy and it's far from it. Easy, I mean."

"It's my understanding that you were accused of something that you didn't do. So you were fired and took off to parts unknown. Correct?" She nodded and then told him that she'd been in trouble before, but this time was different. "This time, it was Tellus who blamed you directly. See? I do pay attention sometimes. When there is not a beautiful naked woman in front of me."

"Yes, so, Tellus got her underwear twisted up about an uprising. And not just any uprising either. The earth's underground had decided that they could do a better job running the upper levels of the earth than Tellus was. They thought, with them running things, that it would be better for them to get what they wanted. Which if you think about it, it was never going to work for them. That to rule beneath the soil, they would be able to keep beings from trampling on their domain. Think about that for a moment. They didn't want people, other creatures, and beings walking on the earth that was their right to do. It was to make their area easier to run. I'm not entirely sure how they thought that was going to work, but I went and took care of it. But, since I killed the ruler, the king of the underground that was in charge before David, I had to be in charge, so to speak, for a few hours while Tellus was able to find someone to take care of the area. Instead, she thought that I had killed the king and queen in order to take over her reign."

"I'm assuming that you explained this all to her." He got a look and decided that it was just too cute for him to comment on right now. She would tear him a new ass, he thought. "Okay, so you explained, she was still pissed off and fired you. I'm still confused as to why that has everyone in an uproar."

"Because I was in charge for about an hour and a half. People and other beings took exception to that because they thought that I'd run it in a way that wouldn't be in their favor. I believe it was just a way for me to get into trouble so that I'd no longer be a warrior. But I don't know that for sure. I didn't want to be in charge, so I let her fire me. I went off and licked my wounds. I did hear later that she found out the truth. Even David, who replaced the king that I killed, told her that it was a mess that took him decades to clean up. But I stayed away. Until recently." He asked her what had brought her out in the open then. "Fran Molder. She was possessed by a being that wanted me to work for her. Now, while I understand wanting me to work for someone other than Tellus, I can't. I was a warrior faerie to her and to her only. This person, I think, wants me to work for her so that she has this inside information about being able to take over the realm. Tellus' realm."

"But you can't be a warrior. Why is that?" She told him. "Okay. That I can understand. If you were a warrior faerie, it would stand to reason that you would rule faeries. And if she doesn't have any, what would you use to fight. This other person, she's a dumbass of the first order."

"I know. But that is where I'm at in all this." He asked about the markings. "Okay, so this mark here, the one that you have too, it's the being that wanted me to work for her. If a marking is in color, as this one isn't, it means she's still alive. Black if dead, as this one is. Red if he was killed by me. Or now, I guess, one of us. I heard from Tellus today. She wants to meet me in the dead being's realm. There will be a mess, no doubt, that will need to be cleaned up."

"You're not going to, are you?" She said that would be up to him. "Why me? I mean...why do I have a feeling that I'm not going to like the reason that it's up to me?"

"You won't. Not if you're smart. This being knew that I had a mate. I guess the world knows that you and I have found each other. But she thought, as most all male beings do that are older than ten years old, that you are the one in charge. You rule the roost." Shiloh said that he didn't rule anything. "No. But you could rule me if you've got a mind to. It's the rules, you see. You're the male to my female. The being thought that you could make me do what he wanted. She would have been correct, too, in her thinking. I would, if you deem it, have to bow before you."

"Nope, not going to happen. Is there…can I just proclaim that I'm not ruling you at all and that you rule me? I like that better anyway." She asked him if he'd really do that. Let her be in charge. "Absolutely. You've been around longer than I have. Not only that, but you've been doing this job a good deal longer than I've been alive, too. I don't know anything about being a warrior. Other than the few times that my family and I fought for lands that needed us to be there for them. I have an idea. Let's see if this will work. I hereby proclaim Roxanna Jarome Golden to be in charge of all decisions pertaining to being in fights, wars, or being a warrior." Shiloh laughed and then pulled her to him. "I belong to you, Rocky. No one else but you. If you want to rule me, then I'm all for it."

"I don't know what to say. I didn't think you'd just say that." He asked her what she had expected him to say. "I don't know, to be honest with you. I just figured that you'd tell me that you had this and that you'd tell me to bake a cake or something. By the way, I don't cook. I could, I suppose, but I don't if I don't have to."

"I know how to cook. I'm pretty good at it, too. But I don't want to cook if it means spending less time with you. I want to get to know you." She laid her head down on his chest, and Shiloh thought that everything was right with the world. "I've been meaning to ask you about something. It's not that big of a deal, but what are we going to do about the Frans of the world. I'm sure there are more than just the one of her if, as you said, they're man-made. That's the boss that was possessed, correct? I know that she's dead now, but I heard that she was man-made. How did that happen?"

"They were sisters, the three of them born to a man and his wife who had no other children. The three of them were evil from the start and created themselves into what there was today. Sadly, the mother, a mage too, but not very powerful, had died birthing the triplets. Which I believe was a good thing. She died a quick death. I think that the daughters wouldn't have made it so easy for her had she lived. I want you to understand that they didn't start out as anything more than mage when they were children. Then, their father, a very powerful mage in his time, was killed. I don't know why or how, but I also don't know that it matters. The sisters, no more than about ten, were left to fend for themselves after their parents were dead. I don't know why that had them turning into what we saw here today, but they were evil even before their father died. By the time they were an entity all into themselves, they were much older and stronger. They perfected their skills by killing small children, children that were younger than their own age, for what turned out to be just simply because they could." Shiloh asked why they'd do that. "The only thing that I've been able to find out when I killed the second sister is that they were taunted by the other children because they were forced to live in the house that had already seen a great deal of murders. Most of them had been done by the sisters, but no one outside the home knew that at the time.

They didn't care for others, not any kind of beings, so they killed indiscriminately. It's believed that they got a taste for it and continued on their paths until they separated. To do more killings, I believe."

"So the last one decides to kill you and, in doing so, drew blood. That alerted others that you were still around, and they decided to get you to work for them. How many people need to be killed before it's apparent that you're not going to work for anyone?" She said that it had been a while since she'd been tracked, but before then had been hundreds. "We need to talk to Tellus. If she were to hire you again, do you think that would keep people from trying to hire you?"

"Doubtful. I don't know if you're aware of this or not, but people are pretty stupid when it comes to greed. I mean, all-powerful and all, it would make even a good person think about trying to get me and now you to work for them for power. And with power comes money. People, in my lifetime, they're stupid when it comes to thinking that they need it all."

"Yes, I've noticed that as well." She sat up and drew her sword as she stood. Shiloh didn't move. He wasn't sure what was going on until Mom appeared on the deck with them. "Mom? That's not a good thing to do when everyone is on edge. You should have warned us."

"I didn't think. I came here because I have some information for you both. I'm sorry, Rocky. Perhaps if we were to share some blood, you'd know it was me when I came around." The sword disappeared, but he noticed that Rocky was staring at him.

"What's happened? Something that I need to take care of?" he didn't move, still not sure what was happening. "Rocky, honey? You need me to do something right now?"

"You didn't move." He asked her what she meant. "When I was ready to kill whatever was coming, you didn't move to try and take over. You meant what you said about not taking over for me. I wasn't sure that I could have believed you, but you meant it, didn't you?"

"Of course I did. I didn't know what was going on and figured that you did better than me. I knew it was my mom, so — you didn't believe me?" She said that she didn't know what to think until just that minute. "I guess I can live with that. All right. Mom? What do you have for us in the way of information?"

"The being that was killed by Allison, did you

know that she was the daughter of a mage by the name of Milton? The name means something to me, but I can't for the life of me remember why?" Rocky told them what she knew of Milton. "That's right. He was supposed to be in charge of all mages back before he was murdered. But his early demise made it so that no one was held accountable after his death for any of the crimes that had been committed by their kind. I remember, too, that he was supposed to have set up better laws that would govern their kind. I don't know that it was ever done, either. Do you think that his daughters killed him? That would go a long way in explaining why his death was so violent. I mean, they never killed anyone without a lot of pain, correct?"

"Yes, that would explain a great deal. I didn't think that it mattered who had killed him, but now that you mention his daughters, it makes sense. They should have been tried for his death along with that of the people of their town. Hundreds of children lost their lives over the decades because of those three." Shiloh asked what it would matter now that they were all dead. "Only in that they would be stricken from the books as mage. If there even was a book around. I don't know. Not that they were only mages at the end of their life, but striking them from the books would mean that their magic would have been purified and given to the families of the people that they killed. It wouldn't have been all that much, I don't guess. Not with all the deaths that they caused, but it might have made the difference between them having a meal or not."

Mom left to get more information, and Rocky paced the deck. She was good at it, he realized. Not pounding the deck like he might well have but gliding across the deck in a smooth motion. When she suddenly stopped and looked at him, he felt his cat snarl. Like it was preparing for whatever she needed for him to do.

"We're going to have to talk about everything. And soon. There is too much at stake for us to be going about our lives like nothing is going on. It started out that I was going to talk to you about the markings, just to sort of ease you into a life like mine, but I think we're well beyond that now. Don't you think?" He asked her if there was something going on. "Forever. But in the fact that people are going to be coming for us, we need to be prepared. I would like for you to see if you can pull a sword. It will be good to know that you can protect yourself if I need you to."

Since he'd seen her do it twice now, he had a general idea of what he had to do. Thinking about a sword like hers, he felt it fill his hand immediately. It startled him, too, to see thousands of faeries appear around him with their swords drawn and at the ready. Standing up, he moved the sword through the air as he watched the little people do the same.

"They'll be with you forever now." He didn't acknowledge Tellus appearing in the area when she did. Instead, he played with the movements of the blade in his hand. "They'll move with you. See how they move with the sword? They're an extension of it. Of your body, too. If you move, they will as well. Watch when you kneel."

Moving to the yard, he worked with the faeries while Rocky and Tellus sat together talking. He didn't know what they were saying, but it didn't seem to be bad. Twice, he saw them laughing, and once, he saw Tellus blush. Whatever they were speaking about, he thought it was a good thing.

Tiring of the play, he went to the deck where they were and sat down. Watching the yard, he noticed things that he'd not before. Not only were there more faeries in the yard now, but there were other creatures, too. In addition to the faeries, there were other leopards and lions, too. He saw the two dragons as well, just before Tellus said his name. Rocky had disappeared at some point, but he wasn't worried about her. She could take care of herself if it was necessary.

"I've done as you suggested and rehired her as my warrior. You, too, as a matter of fact. The two of you will be safer now than before. Not that you couldn't take care of yourself before, but this will provide you with more faeries and other creatures that will come to your aid." He stared at her. Not saying anything but watching her face. "You've figured out that she and I aren't on the best of terms. That's entirely my fault. When I pointed that out to Rocky, she agreed. There was never any getting around her when she was in the right. You'll make a good couple. Strong, too."

"She's not that trusting of you yet, is she?" Tellus shook her head and again said it was her fault. "I'm not going to tell you that you're wrong. I don't have enough information to make that call. However, I know what she told me, and she can't lie to me. Did you really think that she wanted to take over your realm?"

"I did. I don't know why I did at the time. When I think back on it, I think I was just…stressed comes to mind. She'd been taking care of the realm without my knowledge for a great many decades before this happened. I should have been more informed about what she was doing, even if it was after the fact. But I didn't pay any attention to her because I didn't think I had to. Then, she killed the king and his mate of the underworld. To save me. Doing what needed to be done without any kind of fanfare. David said that it was surprising to him that no one had noticed sooner what had been going on. He took me to task about blaming Rocky as well. When I went to find her, she was simply gone. I knew her better than anyone else, but things were…I guess you could say that I wasn't thinking clearly, though. That's a lame excuse as well." Shiloh said nothing. There really wasn't anything that he thought he could say to make a difference. "She's a wonderful person. Full of meanness when it suits her, but she'd not cruel. I have regretted my words and actions since that day. And even now, I hate that this has come between the two of us."

"Good. That means that you'll do something about it." He stood up. "You know that I love you like you're my family, Tellus. However, she will come first in all that I do now. If you hurt her again, I will do everything within my power to get back at you. You have my word on this."

"It's no less than I expect from you, Shiloh." He nodded, but before he was able to leave, Tellus asked him if he had a moment. "She's powerful. I know that your family simply gets more powerful all the time, but Rocky is about as if not more powerful than I am. She's had a long time to work with her magic and enhance it. I'd say that when the two of you bond, there will be nothing that can stop the two of you from taking over anything and everything there is that I rule."

"I nor does she want your job. You will need to remember that if anyone comes to you telling you that we're set to do it. I want to be with my mate. Raise babies if she wants any and be a good mate to her. I've no desire to be what you are. I don't even want to think about what it takes to do your job. But neither of us wants what you have. Ever." She said that she believed him. "Good. It might do you a lot of good to remember that going forward, too. You might be able to be a good friend to Rocky if you do."

When he made his way to his house, he stopped

by the kitchen to get a snack. He was suddenly starving. When he entered the room, there were more faeries than there had been in the yard. They were making themselves at home to protect him and Rocky. Grabbing himself a handful of cookies, he made his way to his office. He had plenty to keep himself busy there and knew that if Rocky needed him, she'd call.

Shiloh had a mate. One that he knew was going to be keeping him on his toes as well as happy. As he was putting in the password for his files, he thought of something else. Christ, his mate was beautiful. Not that he needed a second chance to remember that, but seeing her in the nude was something that he'd not thought of seeing just yet. Smiling, he wondered what she'd say if he were to be naked around her. It was something to think about.

It was dinnertime when he finished up with his work. Rocky had been in several times, mostly to ask him a question about the house or the grounds. When she told him that she was taking care of the land that his house was on, he told her that Tellus had done that some time ago. With only a look, he knew that whatever Rocky was doing would be better.

Closing things up, he was surprised to find

his mom in the living room with Rocky. They were having tea. Something that he'd never thought that Rocky would enjoy. When he was asked if he wanted to join them, he said that he was going to pick up something to eat in town as he had stuff to mail and wanted to know if mom was going to join them.

"I think not. I have a great deal of information now that I can work with. To be honest with you, Shiloh, I'd not realized how late it was. Perhaps you should take your little mate out and have a good dinner. Not that it would be as good as anything you could have here, but you'd be able to enjoy each other." Rocky said she was all for staying in tonight. "Good. Then I'll talk to you later about the lands to the west of us. I think you're correct in saying that we should make it into another orchard."

After his mom left them, he sat down on the couch. He wasn't in any kind of hurry to leave just yet and enjoyed the quiet time with Rocky. She told him that she could have the faeries get them something to eat if they wanted, and they could cook them whatever they wanted, too. He was just content to just sit on the couch for now, he told her.

"I've been thinking about a few things that your mom told me. I exchanged blood with her and some of your brothers. I won't be as surprised now when they just show up. But she said that she thinks that there is one more being out there like the sisters." He asked if they had names. "Not that I was ever made aware of. That's funny, don't you think? That their names were never spoken. Could be that it was some kind of taboo. Anyway, about them killing their father. That makes sense. After talking to Zippy, being a mage is on the same order as being a witch in that they have the same kind of rules to follow. Like they can't kill lesser mages than themselves. Killing their father would have given them a great deal of power. And when their mother died, she would have given them some as well. They were doomed from the start. But this other being out there, he could be trouble for us."

"More than the sisters were?" Rocky said considerably more. "All right. Tell me what you need for me to do and—"

"Did you warn Tellus to be nice to me?" He said that he'd warned her, but nice was never mentioned. "She said that you also told her that we have no designs on her realm. That if anyone said that we were, then she was to know that it was a lie."

"That's right. I'm assuming nothing has

changed since we spoke about it." She said she didn't want it. "All right. Then tell me why you've brought this up now. Has something happened?"

"If Tellus ever becomes incapacitated in any way, we will be required to run the realm until someone can take over for her." Shiloh said that he'd not known that. "I didn't think that you did. But power for power, if it comes to that, we're the strongest to protect it if she can't for some reason. It *was* your mom. However, I don't think she knew that either. But it will be the two of us if anything should happen."

"In what way would that happen?" Rocky didn't answer him, and he wasn't entirely sure that he wanted her to have an answer for that. "I guess that when the time comes, if it does, then we'll cross that bridge when we come to it."

"Pretty much." She stood up and smiled at him. "The thing that I'd like to do is eat dinner, then fuck your brains out. I know that it's short notice and all, but do you think you'd like that?"

"Yes." He stretched out his legs to give his cock more room. "You're not teasing me, are you? I'm a man on the edge right now. The thought of ravishing you has me thinking that making love with you is going to be epic."

"You bet your sweet ass it's going to be epic. Let's have dinner first. You'll need your strength." He wasn't sure what he wanted to say other than he could eat later. "No. We need to eat first. I don't want any distractions when I take you to my bed."

He followed her to the kitchen. When food was set in front of him, he couldn't have said what it was, even if a gun was pointed at his head. But he ate it. Even dessert, too. Again, he didn't know what he was putting in his mouth, but since it wasn't making him ill, he didn't care. He was going to make love to his mate, and that was more than he could have hoped for today.

Chapter 2

Brindle flowed through the air, watching people. The signature that he was looking for was much stronger in this little town than anywhere he'd been before. It could have been his mother and aunts, but he had thought that the aunts were all dead now and wasn't sure that he'd still feel them around. When he found his mom, and he would, he was going to make sure she knew just how displeased he was about how she'd left him.

There were several hundred people out and about today. Yesterday afternoon into the evening, he'd been looking for a place to hide. Brindle didn't need much space now that he was a specter, a whisp his mother called him. But it was still nice to have some kind of roof over his head when the wind blew. It would scatter him to the winds, and he'd have to gather himself up again. That would expend his energy too much, and he'd just drop where he was without any thought to people stepping on him and through him.

It shouldn't have been like that, that he was so subpar about the way that he carried himself. Once he'd been created, he should have been able to make himself a solid or a stronger air so he'd be held together. But his mother had to do the spell three times even to get him to this point. Terrified if she tried it again, he just knew that he was going to be nothing but air, unable to do much of anything. As it was, there were things that he still couldn't do. Like, become solid. He didn't have much in the way of magic, and he had no way to carry weapons or armor either. He was so disappointed in her that he could scream. It wasn't as if he could have killed her. Perhaps, he thought to himself, that was her plan all along. To keep him from killing her.

He could hold his shape for several minutes. But then his magic would be so depleted that he'd have to rest for hours, if not days on end, before he could move again. Parts of his body would just flitter away while he rested, and that would make it so that it took him longer to heal. His mother had been a cow in her magic. Even when she was willing to kill for him, she never got that right. Brindle paused outside of a building that he'd never seen before.

A pair of women came out of the building as he was staring at it. He didn't know that they could see him until they spoke. It was their laughter that had his temper flaring up. When he moved toward them, another being, one that he hadn't any idea what she was, appeared too.

"Hello, Brindle. My goodness, you've certainly been busy." One of the witches, he knew what the first two women were now. She said that he was the son of the now-dead sisters. "A child of theirs? I hadn't any idea that they'd allow anyone close enough to them to breed, much less have sex with someone. Who is your father, Brindle? Or were you created by them?"

"If you mean was there sex, then no, there wasn't anyone that had done the nasty to them. They wanted me and went to find someone that could make me. My mother isn't dead. I saw her just the other day." The person he didn't know let lose some of her magic, and he could taste her power. "You. You're the being that killed one of my aunts. I don't blame you for that. They were, like my mother, ignorant of magic. Not like I am."

"You're ignorant too if you think you can come here and cause trouble. Why don't you go away and fade out? The world in general will thank you for that." Brindle got closer, not too close. He knew that they'd try to harm him. But he could smell something on the stranger. She had a mate. "Come a little closer, Brindle. I'll help you along in your needing to rest forever this time."

"Nay, I shall not. And you cannot harm me because I've done nothing to warrant you harming me. I studied the laws of our kind. You cannot harm anything that hasn't harmed you first." She asked him if he only used that rule when it suited him. Of course, he did. Didn't everyone? "I didn't harm you. If you were to tell me what you are, then we can perhaps work something out. I'm looking for a female warrior to work for me. Do you know of such a being? I will train her to do my bidding as she is only a female."

Brindle was knocked back when the being drew her sword and aimed at him. She was here. The very one that his mother had told him to find. The warrior of the queen of the earth was standing right in front of him as well. And she had a lord over her. A mate he could and would control was perfect for what he needed. Men, he'd come to realize, stuck together about such matters.

"Where is he?" The witch asked who he might be talking about. "The mate to the warrior here. Where is he so that I might have a word or two with him about a job? I have no desire to get myself into any conversation with the likes of you three. We all know that the men are the ones that make the decisions. It's why my mother and aunts were so willy-nilly about their magic. Until I came along, there was no one to temper them."

"If you say so. But our mates understand that we're more powerful than them and are all right with it." Brindle couldn't help it. He laughed. "Ah, so you don't believe us. Well, here comes the warrior's mate now. You can ask him what he thinks about which one of us is going to be talking to you."

He was repulsed by the kiss the two people had. It made the man weaker in his eyes that he'd do something like that. Not just out in the open, but he more than likely did it behind closed doors as well. When two other beings showed up, mates he presumed to the witches, he thought that things were finally going to go his way. However, he didn't understand why they, the men, stood behind their mates. Then it occurred to him. They wished to put then in line of fire first. These men were much more cunning than even he was. He was drawing power from the area around him when the laughter again distracted him.

"You honestly think they'd put us in front of them to draw your fire first? You're about as dumb as your mother was. And she is dead, Brindle. She was killed by a phoenix just this morning." He said that there were no more phoenix left. "You sure about that? I mean, there are the two of them, and last I heard, they were trying to have a child. Another phoenix."

"They're breeding now. Twins, as a matter of fact. I can't wait to see them when they're born. Do you know if they'll just be birds at first, or do they shift later?" The warrior said they would be birds for the first year. "Oh, that's so good to know. I won't buy any baby things then. Just...I'll pay for worms to be in abundance for a gift for the new parents. What do you—"

"What are you going on about? There are no more phoenix." Then suddenly, there were two of them standing in front of them all. Their heat and power so much that he backed away so that he'd not be sucked into their flames. That was the thing about air. He could be sucked into things that would change him. "So? There are two of them. Is this display supposed to impress me?"

"Impress you? Doubtful that it would. But just to show you that you don't know nearly as much as you think you do. And the phoenix that killed your mother, she's before you. Why don't you ask her how your mother screamed out her pain like a child. Ask her how painful her death was. Being burned to death by a phoenix wouldn't be quick. At least it wasn't today. You should get your shit together, Brindle, before you go spouting off shit that you've no knowledge about." He asked the warrior what she was talking about. "The very fact that you're here now, looking for a place to rest, tells me that in addition to you losing your mother and aunts, you've also lost their home. I destroyed it today when I found it. While I only meant to destroy the home and not the property, I'm glad that I did it. You have no rights to the land nor the house that was there. Also, and this might come as a surprise to you, but since we're all here and you've decided that I can be bought, I'm going to tell you that I, along with the people here, are going to kill you. What else have you failed to realize? Well, let me enlighten you some. These men and the three others are children of the woman called Morgan. You know her, don't you? Morgan, Queen of the shifters?"

As the warrior mentioned the people, they appeared in front of the little shop. It was difficult for him to remain where he was as more and more power was brought before him. His stupid whisps wanted to go to where all the power was, and he didn't want that. When she mentioned Tellus, queen of the earth, he tightened his hold on himself. He was beginning to shiver, and that would make parts of him fly away. Then it happened.

Mate to the warrior reached up and took a piece of his whisps out of the air. Brindle couldn't just see his power now but feel it, too. Brindle didn't want anyone to know that to hold a piece of him was—

"I know what it means, Brindle." The man, a very large one at that, came to the forefront and stared at him. "One who holds a piece of you will control you if powerful enough. What do you think? Am I powerful enough to tell you to make yourself into a ball?"

The change was quick and painful. As much as he'd stretched himself out to appear to be more, having to change into a ball showed to them and to himself that he was no bigger than a small ball. Even to a child, he would be considered tiny. The man had him change into several things, one right after the other, while he held onto his part. It was beyond exhausting, and he needed to find a place to rest now. But he couldn't allow that monster to have a part of him.

"Give it over. You've no right to pluck me from the air as if I weren't more powerful than you." He wasn't, and when the male and the others laughed, it was all he could do to hold onto his temper. "Release me, and I'll not harm you."

"Sure you won't. And I think that I'll hold onto this for a while. So long as you're running around freely, there could be trouble. But with this little piece of you, thankfully not too large, or there would be nothing left of you, I can control you. Hear your thoughts, too." He looked at his mate, and Brindle felt sickened by the feelings coming off of them once again. When he looked back, Brindle thought that he discovered something else. "You can't stand love. Or affection, I'm thinking. Since you were created with hate, the opposite can harm you. Is that right? And don't lie to me."

"It weakens me. Whoever gave the thought to tell someone not to lie to them is an idiot. Why would you make it known that you can compel people not to lie to you? That's just a dumb bit of magic that harms those of us that lie to suit ourselves." They laughed at him again. "It's not funny, damn it. It's ludicrous to think that it's a good thing. I suppose you use it all the time. That bit of magic to make people tell you the truth. I hate it and demand that it's never used on me again."

"I didn't before this, but I think I will from now on." They were still laughing when he handed his part to his mate. "If you would be so kind, my love, as to take care of this, then I think we'll be free to do what we were planning before this fool showed up today."

"You do know that if you were to destroy this, it would destroy him as well. Unlike us, he's not immortal. He can be killed like any other being without magic." Brindle screamed that he had magic. The warrior said he had so little it barely mattered. "I mean, it's like a human that might have had a relative way back in their line that had enough magic to bring a book to them, and you got less than half of that. You should have had your mother quit when she created you, Brindle. Each time she changed you, at your insistence, you grew weaker. I could take you on right now and not even pull my sword. Even the youngest of witches could kill you without any kind of knowledge of magic. You're, in a word, useless. Not to mention, bound to my mate as he holds a part of you. A part, I'm thinking that you couldn't well afford to lose."

"I demand that he give it back." They didn't laugh this time but did stare at him. It wasn't until he figured out that they were staring beyond him that he did finally turn. The being there was someone that he'd never encountered before, and it scared him enough that he moved closer to the flames of the phoenix. Too close, actually. He could feel large parts of him being separated from his whole self. But it mattered little, he thought. The creature behind him was set to destroy him anyway, he thought. As well as the people behind him.

"You will do as I say, or I shall destroy you." Brindle didn't know if he was speaking to him or not but said that he could only be with a single master. "I am your master. You will destroy the warrior male and bring his heart to me."

"He owns meself." Brindle didn't know what

to do, so he quickly glanced at the people behind him. "You want him. I think it would be easy for you to get to him. As I said, I can't. He has a part of me."

The sensation of being touched was something that he never thought to get used to. The being, using his great hands, grabbed him and split him into five different pieces. It was nearly impossible for him to get back together quick enough, so when he felt the bite of something behind him, Brindle knew a kind of fear that he'd never once in his life experienced.

The warrior sword from the male was at his backside. Moving anyway, in any direction, would have severed his already precarious hold on himself. As he felt the bite of it dig deeper into his whisps, he knew he would have this only chance to live. Moving toward the being in front of him was better than the one behind him.

As soon as he was close enough, Brindle knew he'd been so wrong. The creature sucked him into his body in a single deep breath. It was a sensation that he thought was sickening, not to mention unhealthy. As he rumbled his way through the body of the thing, he figured out three things very quickly. Firstly, he was going to die like this. Secondly, this being wasn't as strong as he was, just large. And thirdly, this thing would also die by the sword of the warrior as it penetrated the flesh right where he was.

Whatever was happening on the outside wasn't too much different than what was going on inside, he imagined. There was blood, or something akin to it, spreading quickly around him. Filling him and the creature with the green slime that sustained him. The smell of rotted flesh also permeated the air where he was. When he saw the sword, the hilt of the thing, run through the being, it tore him into more pieces than he could get back together. Christ, he should have found himself a place to rest before today. Then he'd still be among the living.

~*~

Rocky felt like she had been zapped after the creature was dead. If asked, and she was sure someone would eventually, she would have thought that trolls like the one that Shiloh had killed were no longer around. Larger than life, meaner than hell, and stupid beyond knowing when to breath in and out. And it had very little magic at all to speak of. Just meanness and his girth.

"I feel sick." As soon as Shiloh fell to the ground, Morgan started for him. But she stopped and looked at her while her youngest child threw up. "Rocky?"

"I didn't do this." Morgan said that she knew that. "Then what's with the look? I mean, you look pissed off at me."

"No. I'm not mad at either of you. But I know why he's ill. Do you?" Rocky said that he was evolving into what she was. "That's right. He'll never have to eat again. Not that he can't, but he won't need to. When he killed this being, he took on some of the magic that it had. It made him ill to have to purify it before he could use it. Is that right?"

"Yes. He won't be ill again from what he's doing. Just this first time. He and I, he'll be better once we bond." Morgan looked at Shiloh as he laid back on the cool grass. "I won't hurt him, Morgan. I promise you that. But this, this is something that needs to happen to make him stronger. And he'll need to be."

"I know that too. I don't have to like that he will change and evolve, but I know it must happen." Rocky took a few paces toward Shiloh before turning back to Morgan when she spoke again. "I don't have to tell you this, but I will. I love him, Rocky. He's owned a piece of my heart since the day he was born. Moreso than the others. He shouldn't be here now. He was…he should have died. He was so small.

Golden's litter of six was the largest she had, and it took its toll on Shiloh. I had to help feed him when he was tiny, and that gave us a bigger bond than I had with the others. Shiloh is more my son than the others simply because we saved each other, I think."

"He won't die, Morgan. You know that, too." She said that she did, but he was still the baby. "Yes. But he's also the strongest of them all. Even before I came to be his mate, you had to know that he was, even before the mates came along, stronger than the other men."

"I did. I think that they did as well but never commented on it." Rocky told her that was the way that it should have been. "Yes. I was told that as well. That his strength had nothing to do with their order of birth and that Shiloh, for his age, should have been the leap lead. But he didn't want it. I doubt still that he'd take it if offered."

"He'll have enough on his plate now, but should he want to take it over, I'll support him. I think you know that as well." Morgan nodded as she continued to stare at Shiloh. "What is it that you're not telling me, Morgan? There is something, isn't there?"

"Yes." She finally looked at her. "Tellus and

the other kings and queens saved him the day he was born. Shiloh is more a part of the world than even I am. Each of them and myself gave him a bit of ourselves to keep him alive. In doing so, it has made him what he is today. A stronger leopard, yes, but he's also magically stronger than most of the people that you will serve."

"Good." Morgan laughed and asked her why that was good. "Because when he stands with me, no matter what we're up against, I know that he'll have the power and magic to do what needs to be done without me telling him."

"You think that because they gave a bit of themselves to him that he'll know how to use their magic." Rocky said that he already knew how to use their magic. "You've seen him do this? Not even I have seen him use anything other than what was given to him by being the first shifter."

"He controls the elements. Not only that, but he's knowledgeable about what he has to do to make things work for him. How did he know, do you think that to take a part of Brindle would bind them together, Shiloh as the master to the whisp. I didn't tell him that. He knew it. Also, to have it would make it so that he could control the thoughts and actions of Brindle. Again, I didn't know that. Then there was the troll. How did he know how to kill this particular kind of troll? He is, as you can see, much different than the other trolls around here and even in the other kingdoms. I would have stabbed him in the heart, but he knew to stab his mouth to kill him. Without that knowledge, we might not have come out unscathed like we did. Also, you might want to think about this too. How did he know that in order to kill them both, he only had to blow the whisp into the mouth of the troll to be able to control them both? Do you think that the knowledge came to him when he needed it? No, not as quickly as he made it work. He knew. I'm sure that if asked, he'd just tell you that he remembered it from somewhere or a book he might have picked up. Morgan, he's beyond brilliant. And that is what makes him so powerful. His brilliance is going to save us all." She asked if they were in danger. "Aren't we all in danger all the time? I mean, it could be something so simple as falling down and breaking something. But with him around, powered up by me as his mate, we'll never have to fear anything again. Not even Tellus, for all her wisdom and power, isn't as brilliant thinking as Shiloh."

Rocky sat down on the cold grass and held Shiloh's head on her lap. She made them a small fire, just large enough that it would keep the two of them warmed up while Shiloh held her hand. Morgan came and sat with them. She only needed to enlarge the fire a little bit to accommodate her, too. As they sat there waiting, Rocky watched as the others, all ten of them, cleaned up the mess that killing the troll had made.

"I saw it in his mind before he died that there are no more like him. Thankfully." Both she and Morgan laughed with Shiloh. "He knew, at the end, that he'd been misinformed about the strength of this family. I didn't get a chance to see who he was talking about, but it's one of the kings and queens that Tellus has working for her. And that it worked before. That's all I could find."

"Like it did with me?" Shiloh said he didn't understand that part that he'd seen, but he'll think on it. Sitting up, she asked him if he was rested. "I'm rested more than before, but not enough to let you jump my bones. Tell me again why we had to leave the house when we'd only just gotten to the bedroom."

"I'm out of here." Morgan stood up and smiled

at them both. "I do need to get going. There are any number of things that I could be doing other than listening to the two of you speak about sex. Also, we need to get together again as a family. There are some things that I would like to discuss with the bunch of you that needs to be said as a group. Nothing terrible, but just something that I've been thinking about."

"All right. When?" Morgan said in a couple of days if that was all right with them. Shiloh said he didn't have anything planned, but that had never stopped them from getting together before. "It would be great too if we were to talk about the upcoming fundraisers the school is having for their band trip to New York this year. I understand that they're in the parade again."

"They are. And that's a good thought, too. We've only supported them via a cash sum. This year, they want to have an indoor craft show and get some money from that. We could all share in that, I'm thinking. Write down any suggestions you can think of too about the second orchard as well as the larger pasture for the cows. We have a few more than we did last year, and I'm thinking that selling them on the hoof might help a lot of families that otherwise might not get any meat over the winter months."

"I like that idea." When Morgan left them, the others came to tell them what they were going to be doing the rest of the day. It looked as if all of them were going to be out of their hair for a few days as they were following up on some long-term projects around the country. She just wanted to have sex with Shiloh. He looked at her when everyone was gone. "While I love just sitting here with you, my ass is about frozen to the ground, and I can't feel my toes. How about we take this home."

She took them home and into their living room with her magic. There was a fire in the fire place that was lit, as well as a basket of food for them to enjoy. Rocky told him that he'd need to drink more but wouldn't necessarily have to eat anything anymore.

"Yes. And when I do eat, I should eat more greens than anything. I don't need red meat anymore. Though I do enjoy a nice steak." She said that she did as well, but it wasn't anything that she had had in a long time. "We should grill out soon. Not today. I'm too exhausted to—it's not because I killed those two but my body adjusting to their deaths, correct?"

"Yes. You took on their magic." Rocky explained to Shiloh what had happened when he killed them and how his body had to break down their dark magic so that he could use it. "However, after today's events, you won't be sick again. You've adjusted for that."

They talked about different things. Rocky dozed off and on and always woke to Shiloh staring at her. She could never get an answer from him as to why he was doing that, but he seemed to be happy about it, so she didn't fuss at him too much. Once the sun was down, not even being that late, the two of them went up the stairs again to their bedroom. She didn't know if it was going to be very restful for her, as she'd been dozing for a while, but almost as soon as the lights were out, she was too.

"*Rocky?*" She opened her eyes and looked around the darkened room. Reaching out her hand, she didn't feel Shiloh beside her, but the bed was still warm, so she thought that he was close. The voice speaking to her wasn't one that she knew right away. Like magic was changing it somehow. "*I'm in need of your help. The castle is being overrun again.*"

Sitting up, she reached out but couldn't connect with anyone but the person speaking to her. When Shiloh joined her in the bed, she wrapped her body around his and held him to her breasts. The person speaking to her said that she needed to get to the castle soon, as there were faeries dying and she was under attack.

"I don't know your voice." Shiloh whispered in her ear that he would contact Tellus. *"Who are you, and what kingdom do you run? As I said, I don't know you."*

"Yes, you do. You've been my friend for decades. It's me." Rocky told Shiloh what the person was saying, and he put his hands on either side of her head and his forehead to hers. It was like she'd been amplified with him doing that. *"You have to remember me, Rocky. We've been friends for a very long time. Someone is here now, trying to take over my realm. Can you come here and help me? Please? It's your job, isn't it? To help the other kingdoms?"*

The announcement hadn't been made yet that she and Shiloh were working again for the queen. This person couldn't have known that yet. Asking again what her name was, it finally occurred to her who it was. It was more scary than the king from before. This woman was indeed a good friend of Tellus. It was Holly, the queen of the landscapes. However, she wanted her to think that it was Tellus.

After asking Shiloh to find out if she'd been told, he nodded. While he spoke to Tellus, he could also hear Holly. Her description of the taking of her realm was almost word for word, the description of the king of the undergrounds asking her to come to him so long ago.

Christ, this was going to have her being hurt again. Not physically. Never that. She was too powerful for that. But Tellus could rip her heart out this time, and it would hurt her mentally. She didn't know after all this time if Tellus would believe again that she didn't want her realm. Nor did she want anyone else's place in the realm of kings and queens that were there with her.

"Tellus is on her way to Holly. It's not unusual for them to talk late at night. She's going there to just talk about the day. They're good friends." Rocky asked Shiloh if he thought that Tellus would believe anything that she said. "I don't know. I honestly don't, but we have warned her. Twice that we've no desire to take her place. It will, I suppose, be up to her should she believe her or us. Holly has been around longer than I have. I don't know what to think."

Neither did she, and she wasn't going to take any chances either. Not with this mate. Not with Shiloh and his family. Telling him to tell them all what was going on, she also told them that they'd be hiding out. That the two of them would be going to her home until this was over. She only hoped that Tellus still had no idea where she'd been hiding and what she'd been doing while hiding out. It might be the difference between a good life or one that no one would want anything to do with. Especially her.

Chapter 3

Shiloh was enjoying himself. Perhaps a little too much, but it was fun playing this game of hide and seek. While he knew that Tellus nor any of the others had any idea where the two of them were, he could sit outside late at night and watch the comings and goings of the main castle.

Not only was there no power trip happening, but there wasn't a peep from the landscapes either. All was quiet like it should have been. When he saw the herd of unicorns coming in his direction, he was shocked by the number of them. Thousands of them were grazing the land that he and Rocky were staying on.

When the king of them came close to where he sat, Shiloh made no sudden moves but put out his hand and lowered his head. He would pay homage to the older unicorn in any way he deemed fit for being unannounced on what he figured was their land.

"My lord?" He looked up from his lowered head when someone, more than likely another faerie, spoke from behind him. "He wishes to help you stay hidden with the Lady Roxanne. He said that he is greatly indebted to her and will be forever. Your wish will be his command."

"Can I speak to him directly?" The faerie moved around him and in front of the unicorn king. "Please tell him that I mean no disrespect but would like to speak to him about why we are here."

"Everyone knows why you are both here, my Lord. They've not told anyone of the kings and queens, as we wish to keep you safe. The ones that are sent out to find the two of you are going away from this land, as the unicorns haven't allowed anyone on their land in decades. He, his name is Lew, he said that you will be quite safe here for as long as you wish." She turned back to the unicorn. "He said that you may speak to him should you wish but not to go near the breeding ones. He is fearful that someone like you, who is powerful and large, would frighten them. Lord Lew is correct. As I have said, there have been no other creatures here for centuries."

The cold nose of the unicorn touched his open palm. Nodding once, Shiloh stayed where he was on the ground and regarded the king and his harem. Several of the small ones, no more than a few years old, came to sit on his lap. After getting permission, he petted them while speaking to the king.

"Holly, queen of the landscapes, is trying to take over the queen's realm. We're here hiding out so that Tellus doesn't think that we're a part of her plot. We, neither Lady Rocky nor I, have any desire to be anything more than we are now. Warriors to the Queen Tellus." Lew told him that they all knew that as well. "Good. I don't want anyone here thinking we're plotting against the queen by staying on this land without her knowledge. But this thing with the other queen? I don't think it's going to end well for her."

"Long ago, Lady Roxanne stayed here for the same reasons. To keep an eye on things and to make sure that the kingdom was safe. However, Arnold, the previous king of the underground, wanted to rule. Thinking that he would get things just the way he wanted after killing off the queen. It would never have worked. It was then, just before he was killed and that of his lady wife, that he told Tellus that it had all been the idea of Lady Roxanna. Her mate, Hamish, a sorry excuse for a being agreed with Arnold, and the lady had to kill him as well." That explained a great deal to him, and told Lew that. "I would imagine that she would have told you sooner rather than later, but you have both been so busy. She doesn't—still doesn't trust well. But my harem and I have noticed that she trusts you with not just keeping her safe but with her heart as well. I do not believe she ever gave her heart to her first mate. He would have destroyed her, I think, had she been so foolish."

"I didn't care for the fact that he wanted me to build him a large mansion with plenty of young faeries around to wait on him." Rocky kissed him on the mouth, then put her hand out to Lew. "It's been a long time, my dear friend. I'm happy you've decided to come and speak to my mate. He's a good man. Much better, I think, than I deserve."

"Nah. The two of you are a pair. Match perfectly like my children to their mothers. You are strength alone but power together. You are both well suited." Shiloh thanked the unicorn king. "Think nothing of it."

They spoke about the first mate to Rocky, and

he could tell that she hadn't loved him. From the sounds of it, he could have easily gotten her into so much more trouble had he been able to live. When something occurred to him, he nearly stood up but calmed himself when he woke the babies sleeping in his lap.

"Lew, do you remember Arnold at all?" He said that he did indeed. "Could you describe him for me? What color were his eyes and hair? Was he a large man or somewhat small in stature? How was his wife built and her eyes as well?" Rocky asked him what he was thinking. "More than likely just thinking too much outside the box. But I'm wondering if Holly is making this work for her because she was related to them. There was a child born of them. I got that information when you and I swapped memories. The reports, it doesn't mention that you killed their offspring. Did you?"

"No. I don't remember anyone mentioning the child when I was there to stop the invasion. I do remember now that you mentioned it that there was a child. But I don't know if I knew if it was male or female. You think that Holly is their child?" He said that he didn't know, but it couldn't hurt to check. "No. I suppose not. Damn it. I should have checked on this myself long ago, and this wouldn't be an issue."

Closing his eyes when he was asked to do so by Lew, he sent him image after image of the other man. Turning to Rocky, he could see by the look on her face that she thought that they looked alike as well.

"Holly is Arnold's child." He didn't look at Lew when he asked him if there was a way that he could make sure of what they were thinking. "Smell. She would smell like him. Perhaps that's why she never got close to me when we were here in this realm. Damn it all to fuck and back."

"I will speak to the queen, my lady, my lord. I believe she is well aware that you are here now. Not that any of us have told her, but she sent word to me just this morning to tell me that the fields here needed some trimming. I think, that it is her way of letting us get information to her." Rocky laughed when he did. "She is very slick, my lord. I thought me to be remiss in doing my job, and when I got here, I was sorely confused. But as I said, I think that she knows and is letting me know, too. She is a smart queen, I believe."

"Yes, but will she believe that we've nothing

to do with anything going on is the big question." Lew said that if she did not, he would poop in her castle and have his harem give birth to the newborns outside her door. "I think that might do it, Lew. Thank you."

As Lew's harem started working on the fields, he lay down in the sun. Shiloh knew that he was speaking to the queen. When she laughed, much like a braying donkey did, Shiloh laughed as well. Even if they weren't blamed for what was going on, he knew there were going to be others who would believe what they wanted. As he was keeping an eye on the unicorns, he also kept a close eye on the castle. Whatever was going on in there, he was sort of nervous about how well Tellus was going to take being told that one of her own — again — was plotting to kill her.

"The queen does indeed know that you are here with the lady, Roxanne. She said that your mother told her and then warned her that she would quit her if she did something stupid once again. When I asked her what that meant to quit someone, she said that Morgan told her that she'd hide out with the two of you and she'd allow gasoline and other nasty things onto the land. I believe her. Lady Morgan is frightful when she is upset, don't you agree?"

He thought it best that he didn't agree or disagree with the unicorn. When he laughed, Shiloh smiled. *"She also said that you'd have nothing to say about that either. I have found out some things. I am speaking to you like this, young Shiloh, because I don't want anyone around me to hear. I believe there to be spies everywhere. Holly is his daughter. However, it was your mother that told me when she did some research. Lady Tellus is beside herself with worry for the two of you, my lord."*

"So long as we come out with no blood shed from us, I can keep myself and lady Rocky safe. Mostly, it will be her keeping me safe. She's a good warrior." Lew said that she was. A great warrior. But he'd not say that to her face to face. *"Yes, I've noticed that as well. She doesn't take praise well."* They both laughed. *"Thank you for your help, Lew. And for the enjoyable afternoon with your children. They're beautiful."*

"You will have great warriors one day yourself, my lord. And my family and I will be there to welcome them to the world with you." Shiloh thanked him again. *"You are very much welcome. Take the feather that I have left for you and your mate and wear it at all times. Just slip it into your hair, and anyone who needs to know will see you as a friend of the unicorns. And we will protect you as our own."*

Shiloh was humbled by the gift. The unicorns were beautiful creatures yet furious when necessary. He'd heard that once a great war was started, and when the unicorns arrived to fight with the foes, the enemy simply dropped their weapons on the ground and left. There had only been the two of them, and it was more than enough to scare off the hundreds that had come to fight that day. That was the kinds of friends he needed in his corner. He and his family.

~*~

The cave where the two of them were staying was nice. The walls remained the same temperature year-round. It was never too hot or too cold. But while living here long ago, she'd made herself a fire pit in order to cook and clean with as well as keep her toasty when the weather turned wet and cool. She was still working on the fireplace she wanted in their bedroom when Shiloh joined her.

"That's really beautiful. I love how you got the stones to be all the different colors of the mountain." He sat down on the side of the bed and watched her walking around. "Lew is going to keep an eye on the castle for a few days, then he and his family need to move deeper into the mountains before the breeding season begins. There are a great deal more of them than I think a lot of people realize."

"There are." He told her that Lew had told him the story as to why he owed her so much. "It really wasn't that big of a deal, and had I thought about it beforehand, there would never have been an issue with the run off from the top of the mountains. As it was, when the flooding happened, his first wife and their children were caught up in the storm and nearly washed away. What did he tell you? I'm sure that it wasn't anything simple."

"He said that you heard their cries and flew right onto the fast-moving water and pulled them to safety. Even giving a bit of yourself so that his mate would live. I believe his story over how simple yours is." She glared at him. "That doesn't bother me as much as you might think. I think you're kind of sexy when you do that."

"You think that me being upset with you is sexy?" He nodded. "Then you're more deranged than I thought. Why? I don't think you're sexy at all, so I don't know why you'd think me being frustrated at you is sexy."

"You don't think that I'm sexy?" She shook her head and then had to look away. He was entirely too sexy, and he knew it. When his hands came from behind her and wrapped around her waist, she held him there, leaning heavily back onto his chest. "What's wrong? Something happened while I was outside? Or are you realizing how much time you're going to have to spend with me now that we're mates?"

"I'm afraid." It wasn't an admission that she wanted to say aloud. But she did. With him, she felt some of her fear spill over her more. Turning in his arms, she laid her head on his chest. "What if she blames me again? Or worse, us. I think I could take her being upset with me more than I could with her being upset with you. Your mother would have a cow and might get hurt. Then your brothers because, well, she hurt their momma. And all the time, you and I are in hiding again because she couldn't get her head out of her ass and have a look around."

"You certainly do run from hot to blazing, don't you?" He laughed and pulled her back into his arms when she tried to get away. "I have faith that she's not going to believe anything that Holly says. To be honest with you, I think that she'll be twice as hard on Holly than she might have been if not for the fact that she doesn't want you hurt again. As for hurting my mom? That's not going to happen. Like myself and my brothers, I think she is terrified of Mom, and with good reason. Mom is fucking scary when backed into a corner."

"Did she tell you about your birth?" Shiloh said that she had, several times over the years. "Whenever I think about you almost dying, it hurts my heart so badly. She said that you're her baby. I don't know what she's looking at when she calls you that, but you're a grown assed man, and she needed to get her eyes tested."

"She knows that we're men. I hope anyway." His fingers danced up and down her spine, making her relax more than she had been in a long time. "When I was just a small kid, I really was the runt of the litter. She took me out to the far pasture and showed me where her parents were laid to rest. She never said anything about them, not in all the years since then, either. We just sat there for about an hour, saying nothing to each other. When she finally turned to me, she told me how they'd come to die. How, in their effort to kill her off, they had missed their shot because of my biological mother."

"She killed the men that were after her. Her parents had sold her to a bunch of men to rape and kill when they were finished. I heard that story a long time ago. I wasn't sure that it was true or not." He said that it was. More than likely more gory than she'd made it out to be. "She brought Golden here, and the staff took care of her until she was old enough to do it on her own. I can't imagine a time when Morgan wasn't able to care for herself."

"Yes, me either. She's always been our rock." He didn't say anything for several minutes, then started again. "Mom told me that they had died, and since she was still alive, she was able to inherit their estate. Even for as long ago as it was, it was quite massive. What you see here today is from Tellus telling her when to invest in things and when to sell. It was cheating, but since she was able to help so many others like Golden, she didn't mind that one cheat. As the years went by, she understood how to do it on her own. Teaching us, particularly me since I was so ill when I was born, how to buy and sell things to make and have money."

She looked up at him. "What is it that you're trying to work around the bushes to tell me? I'm sure that there is something there that I'm either not getting or I don't want to get it." He kissed her on the nose. "That might work for others but not for me."

Grabbing a handful of his balls, quite an

impressive set of them, too, he rocked into her hand and moaned. There wasn't any way that she was going to give him pleasure while he was talking to her. But she just couldn't take her hand away. Even as she moved up his shaft, it was getting harder with each passing second. She knew that she was going to be in trouble here if they continued.

It took her three tries to get her voice to work correctly. The first time, she was hoarse and couldn't speak beyond a few words. The second time, she moaned. Several times as he continued to fuck her hand. Christ, she was going to die right here from the pleasure of this man. When she finally was able to speak, he leaned over her and nipped at her shoulder. The pain and pleasure of it was so intense that she had a climax. Two of them before she could finally ask him what he was talking about.

"We're wealthy. Very much so." He worked his way around her throat to her ear lobes. "Billions upon billions of dollars are ours to do with what we wish. However, all I can think about right now is how much I want to lay you out on the bed here and eat you."

"I have money too. Not…please, I can't think." He told her that thinking was overrated and that she should just go with the flow. "If I do that, then we're not going to be leaving this cave for days, if not years. I need you."

"I love you, Rocky." She looked up at him, her heart pounding in her chest from his declaration of love to her. "I have loved you since you stood before me with a sword in your hands. I will continue to love you long after that sword has been retired. You are my heart. My reason for breathing and the only reason that I will ever love someone from now until eternity."

"I love you too." She looked up at him and smiled. "Do you suppose you could talk less and figure out something else to do with that beautiful mouth of yours? I mean, I could suggest a few things if you think that you're up for it." She screamed when he picked her up and swung her around the room.

Dropping her on the bed, he was quick to follow her and growled when she tried to get away. Teasing him was the best, she thought. His growls were as sexy as fuck, and she couldn't have needed him more.

As he kissed his way down her body, she let him. Both of them could have been naked in seconds, but it was more fun for him to strip her nude. Each layer of clothing, even her socks that she'd had on to keep her feet warm, removing them sent a shiver of pleasure through her that was incredible.

"There is so much of you for me to explore. The tiny little scars that you have intrigue me. The larger ones make me want to hunt down the person who gave them to you and avenge you. The small mole you have here. The tiny sigil that's here." He kissed each place that he mentioned, even licking along the long line of sword scars that she received long before she'd ever met him. When he'd come across a marking, one that had been a battle or a siege, it tingled along her body like he'd sent a shockwave throughout her heart and soul. Christ, she knew that she wasn't going to last long if he was this methodically about her.

Her body ached. Not in a painful way, though, but in a way that made her realize how alive she was. How tender her body had become under his hands. Each time that he touched her, another part of her would wake. Tingle a little, then feel regenerated. Then he slipped her pants off with her panties.

She could smell her own arousal. Even as her thighs became wet with her need, Shiloh licked her inner thighs as he slid his hand up between her legs to her bottom. While he held her up, holding her just at his mouth, she couldn't have looked away if her life had depended on it. She needed to see him take her. And take her he did.

Screaming out her release, she held onto the bed, digging her nails deeply into the mattress until she knew her fingers would tear at the material. When he licked her a second time, then put his mouth over her pussy, every part of her body seemed to tense up until she let go of the most primal scream. It was as if she were announcing to the world that she was coming. It felt like that as well.

Shiloh ate her for what seemed like hours. Fucking her with his fingers and tongue had her dizzy from the releases. Each time she thought that she'd had enough, he would begin anew, and she'd be flying higher and higher. Only to drop over the edge of ecstasy quicker and more violently. Finally having had enough, her body feeling abused, she pulled him from her pussy and stared at him.

His face was covered in her creamy juices. His lashes and the tips of his hair were as well. When he licked his lips, never taking his eyes off of her, she came again, just throwing back her head and letting her body once again enjoy the fabulous things that he was doing to her. His soft laughter had her panting, waiting for his next move. When he stood up, his body hard and lean, she licked her own lips when she saw how engorged he was. How his cock, longer than her forearm, stuck straight from his body. Before he could move toward the bed, she wrapped her hand around his width and was both afraid and excited that her fingers would touch.

"I need to taste you." He shook his head, telling her that he was much too close for that. "Then later. Fuck me, Shiloh."

"My pleasure, my heart." She laid back on the bed, her body tight with anticipation. She wasn't a virgin; she'd been around a very long time, but she felt like one right now. Her body was his, and she wanted him to enjoy her as much as she had him. Then as he made his way up her body again, she watched as he held his cock in his hands. "I need you."

All the foreplay that they'd had didn't prepare her for the moment his cock filled her. He didn't slam into her as she thought that he would but instead slid into her inches at a time. His cock pulled and stretched her, filling her sheath with all of him. When he slammed forward after she dug her nails into his back, neither of them moved for what seemed and eternity and a half.

Between his body and his hands, Rocky felt like there was nothing of her that he'd left untouched. Her breasts were teased and tormented. Her hips were lifted and held. Even her earlobes were nibbled upon to the point where she was sure it was the most erotic part of her body.

As his movements became more, so did his hold on her. Each time he fucked her, she came closer and closer to feeling like this climax was going to be the end of her. Holding onto her, he told her that he needed to come, and she dug her nails deeper into his skin. Then, when she could feel his movements getting more erratic, she wrapped her legs around his hips and hung on. Christ, she could feel every drop of his cum as it entered her.

It filled her quickly, she knew. The heat of it, the way that it kept coming, had her begging, not for him to stop but to give it his all. And he did. Fucking her through two more climaxes that took her breath away until his groin banged against her clit one more time.

The room didn't darken as she slipped away. There was a brightness about it, stars and unicorns dancing above her head. Even when she closed her eyes tightly against all the color, she could see it. As she began to slip under the spell of coming with her one and only true love, Rocky felt her body come apart in pleasure and slam back together once more before she let herself go.

Chapter 4

Shiloh lay there for several minutes as his body continued to have little deaths. He'd never understood that saying before, that climaxes were called little deaths until just now. The last little death felt like it had indeed killed him. He turned to look to make sure that Rocky was all right and had to laugh a little.

Her long hair was tangled up around her head just so that he could see her nose and some of her eye. With her eyes closed, she looked like a dream. But her soft snores, not anything that he'd tell her that she did, amused him so much that he reached over and ran his finger down her soft cheek. Her mumbled 'leave me alone' had him laughing harder. Then, when it looked like she was going to be out for a while more, he got up and dressed himself, only to go outdoors and have his cat take him. It was like he'd been waiting for the opportunity to be out of doors just so that he could take his body.

It was strange. He was his other half, yet he seemed to have no control over him. It was as if he were two of the same being. Shiloh knew that one of his brothers could do that, shift so that he was two different people but not him. Besides, he was himself, just…well, without control. As he moved around the grounds where they'd been staying, stretching out his claws both front and back into the rich earth, Shiloh kept an eye on the area around them. It wasn't a good time to have someone sneak up on them without him having any idea if he could have his cat save them.

When his body just dropped to the ground, he had just a moment of fear until the cat stretched out again. He'd been terrified that he'd been hurt, or worse yet, they were all under attack. This time, it was like he was trying to make his muscles longer, stronger even. Then, as it seemed as if he were as stretched out as far as he could go, he tossed back their head and dug his claws deeper into the earth. Feeling his back pop in several places, he hadn't realized how tense he was until that very moment. Lying back down, he felt better than he had in years.

Shiloh didn't know what was going on, but

he could feel the cat's presence more than ever. As his muscles began to move, just with the simple movement of his waist and body, he felt larger. Not just with his muscle mass but his height and weight, too. While feeling really good about his new improvements, he was still just a little nervous about why these things were going on with his body.

As he was trying his best to get a handle on what was happening, he felt his shoulders begin to ache. Not painfully, but just like he might have pulled a smaller muscle, and it needed to be massaged. Before he could roll to his back, even if he thought that his cat would listen to him, he felt a quick searing pain in the scapula in his back, then nothing more. Like whatever it had been had done its damage and had left. He turned when he heard something behind him. Shiloh was relieved to see that it was Rocky. But honestly, she looked odd to him. He couldn't quite put his finger on what it might have been either.

"I felt it." He asked her what she had felt. "Your connection to the earth and to myself. I didn't know what it was until I just saw you. How are you doing? I have to say, you look fantastic. It's like you've been blown up a bit here and there. How do you feel?"

"I don't know. I feel clumsy and odd — you're

little. That's it. You look so tiny." She laughed, and he wondered at that, too. *"Help me. I haven't any idea what is going on, and I'm slightly afraid. I can't figure out what is going on. Also, I feel as if I don't have any control over myself."*

"That'll change, I'm sure. As for me being tiny, no. It's not me. It's all on you this time. It's you that is larger. I'm talking like way larger than even an elephant. I'm sure that once you think about it, you'll understand that you're bigger all over. Not just your muscles but your paws, head, and even your tail are a great deal bigger than you were before we bonded. And you have wings. They're still coming out, but you're going to have them." He tried to look over his shoulder to see them, but he kept falling over things. "Just calm down a little. You're going to cause a lot of damage to the forest if you don't just settle down. Okay. Let me give you a visual of what I see when I look at you. Okay. I've looked at you. Now, you close your eyes, and you should be able to see what I see when I look at you."

Closing his eyes, he could see himself. That didn't help him much until he noticed the trees that had been growing outside the cave that they'd been staying in weren't right. They were small, like twigs leaning against the rock walls. Even the opening of the cave looked about a quarter of the size that it had been. Watching Rocky now, gently and slowly moving his front paw towards her, he was shocked to see that she was about the size of one of his claws. One of his very sharp and deadly-looking claws. He thought of the damage that he could be doing to her, and it again terrified him.

Taking his hand back, sliding it under his body, he laid his head down beside her. Standing up, she was about as tall as he was at eye level. Afraid to even breath around her, thinking of the damage that he might do to her, he used their link to ask her what was going on.

Instead of answering him, he watched as she called forth the faeries. When they disappeared so quickly, he was terrified that they were going to go and get someone to kill him off. When he felt the smack to his mouth, he turned and looked at Rocky.

"Stop thinking that you're going to be hurt by me. Christ, this is awesome if you think about it. Have you figured it out yet?" He asked her if she was talking about him having a heart attack all the time. If not that, then he had no idea. "You're my ride."

When the faeries returned, they put something

on his back. While they were telling him where to move and how to do it, his mind kept repeating what she'd said to him. He was her ride. A ride to go where? The faeries were finished with whatever they were doing, and he was told to lie down. When he did, Rocky climbed up on his back. It was by and far the strangest thing that he'd ever felt. The smallness of her climbing over him like he was nothing more than a jungle gym, and she was a child set on scaling him. That, finally, was something that he could laugh about. Him being big enough for her to climb, and he was willing to allow her to do that.

"All right, Shiloh, let's start out slowly. You should know how to use your wings, Correct?" He did and told her that. But he still didn't know what he was doing with wings. "You'll be fine once we get this going. Just fly with me, and I'll be right here."

He knew that in order to take flight—which he was still trying to figure out—he needed to start running. As he made short work of the forest floor, his wings, or what he had thought were his wings, started to move. In seconds, not only was he in the sky, but he'd never felt anything better in his life. It was the most powerful and freeing thing that he'd ever encountered. His body, even for a big as it was as a human, was now soaring through the sky like one of the little faeries that he'd come to depend on of late. And oh holy Christ, what a view he had.

Paying attention to his surroundings had never meant so much to him as they did right now. While he wasn't high in the sky, there were things that would pop out at him as he skimmed along the tree tops. A flock of birds nearly had him crashing to the ground, trying to avoid them. Then, another time, it was a bunch of sheep from the ground that startled when he came out of the tree line. He didn't know who was more surprised, him or them. So he flew just a bit higher so that he could see the things that Rocky was telling him to look for.

The tops of trees were so beautiful that he thought he could fly over them forever. It wasn't just a forest of greenery as he'd thought. But individual trees with pointed tops in some areas and rounded, wonderfully full trees in other places. Bare patches of ground gave way to waterways and more trees. There were animals, large and small, running through the forest that watched them as they flew overhead. It was the most epic thing that he'd witnessed in some time. And all the while, he got to share it with his one true love, Rocky.

As they flew around for about an hour, he found himself getting used to what he could do. Not only could he hang onto mountain sides, but he could also carry things with him. Large boulders were one of the many things that Rocky had him working with. He didn't even care that a couple of the thoughts that he'd had on the usage of the large rocks were scary and bloody.

He flew over the town—Rocky made it so that no one would see them as they flew around—and he could see how much the town needed in the way of new roofs on homes. Yards needed to be built up, too. There were several that he'd not noticed from the ground that he could see were covered in tarps. Tarps in as poor shape as he'd ever seen.

Yards should have been in full bloom this time of year, but he could see where patches of the earth were too barren to sustain even a blade or two of grass. They'd need to get some of the faeries there so that they could sort things out for those people. Make it so that the yards for most of these people would hold a seed to grow or even a bush to brighten up a corner with flowers or berries. There were trees that needed to be trimmed. Also, waterways that were blocked up with downed trees were also causing the water to rise dangerously close to the houses, which might flood them out. As he made a mental list of the things that he could see, his mom reached out to him.

"*I just saw the strangest thing fly over. Is it you, my dear boy?*" His laughter must have been answer enough for her because she laughed too. "*My goodness. You look like a plane going over. I can tell that this form of you is going to be very helpful for everyone around.*" He told her of the things that he was already thinking to be worked on.

"*I also think that Rocky and I are going to be helping out the realm around the castle for Tellus, too. With my size and ability to fly and Rocky's magic and her abilities, I think that there won't be too many coming around to mess with her once they get a look at us. The simple fact that I can fly should keep others out, but you just never know about creatures anymore.*" She asked him where Rocky was. "*She told me that the faeries made her a harness. She's riding on my back right now. Mom, this is the coolest thing ever. Telling me what she thinks that I need to do so that we're a powerful couple. Mom, I have wings.*"

They both laughed again, and Rocky told him that he needed to settle down to the earth, that Tellus was looking for them. After telling his mom what was going on, he landed in the forest, lying down so that

Rocky could crawl down from him. But she spread out her own wings and alighted on the ground like a gentle breeze, landing on her feet without so much as a twig breaking the silence. When she was next to him, he felt his own wings curl around him, and he saw that while he was still bigger than he'd been before, he was no longer a monster that towered over Rocky. She warned him not to say a word to Tellus about his newfound magic. He didn't know why that was important to her, but he'd do whatever she needed of him.

"There you are." He shifted from his cat to his human self and was dressed when he did. Of course, he could do this before, but it seemed quicker to him. Not paying attention to Tellus, he had to ask her to repeat herself. That he'd been thinking about other things. "I'm sorry. I should have greeted you first. But I'm glad that I've found you both well. I have a feeling that things are starting to heat up in the world with Holly. As you can well imagine, all the other kings and queens are taking this hard. No one suspected her to be like her father. Or even who her father was. I hate to admit this, but I should have done more research on her before taking her under my wings."

"Yes, you should have. But that's it's done now, so let's move on. What is it you want us to do?" Rocky sat down next to him on the ground while Tellus sat in the oversized chair that she had made for herself. Tellus asked if they had been here long. "No. Not really. We've been exploring. But we've also been hiding out. If you're here to tell me that you're going to make this all on us, then I'm going to disappear so quickly that—"

"I'm not. I swear to you, I'm not going to blame anything on you or Shiloh." The faeries brought them drinks and plates of sweets, and Shiloh realized just how thirsty he was. "I went to speak to Holly last night. I didn't think anything would be upsetting about it. We used to do it a great deal before Morgan's family started to grow. I have so enjoyed all the new people and the—Never mind. Anyway, she seemed upset with me when I got there. I think it took her a good hour before she got her temper under control. As it was, all she kept telling me was that she'd had a very busy day and that she didn't mean to take it out on me. Then we talked about the issues that are going on with the surrounding areas and how much the winter is going to take its toll on the landscaping. Just usual business things like we usually discuss.

When we were finished up, she again seemed annoyed with me, so I left. But there are a couple of my warriors there to keep an eye on things with her. I find this part truly sad, but I'm not having any trouble at all seeing her in this new light. It's almost as if I have a clearer picture of her than I ever had. I've also taken to notice that she isn't as friendly with the other kings and queens either. She'll talk to them, but she's not nice. I think that's been going on a lot longer. I just never realized it before. Blinded by my own what I thought was a good friendship. Joel told me that she's short with him every time he goes to see her and hates to be around her, too."

"Last week, when we were making plans for the spring planting for the other realms around here, she told my mom that she didn't need to set up too many things like that. It would be a waste of time. I think Mom laughed it off, but now that I think about it, she was serious. I think Mom realizes that as well. That Holly has been planning this, whatever she's doing, for some time now, and like you said, it's coming to a head with her." Tellus said that at least since, thankfully, her father had been killed. "Yes. I would imagine that she's had to work her way around a lot of things to get where she is today. I'm thinking that when we do go to her realm, we're going to find a lot of bodies. I doubt very much she just got to where she is by doing a good job."

"Sadly, you're right, Shiloh. I've done some digging on my own and have found mass graves of the smaller creatures around my kingdom, too. It hurt me terribly to find out how many were killed by her hand. Once I found them too, the ones that survived her have been coming forward and telling me of the other things she's been up to. For instance, she's been gathering her own army of trolls and the like. The one who was killed recently—through no fault of his own, as it turned out—had been beaten so much that he went mad with the pain. That was the reason that he attacked. I have a feeling once we go to her lair, we're going to find a lot of that sort of thing going on. Her stealing resources as well as weaponry. Speaking of which, I've had the armory sealed up until further notice. Rocky, do you think that you could go there for me after this is over and figure out what we've lost?" Shiloh mentioned that he'd done it last night.

"Since I don't sleep, as you know, I roamed around looking for things that I could get into. I can tell you what you've lost right now. It's more than

I think that even you can imagine. I know that it shocked me. Also, seeds have gone missing as well. A great many of the old saplings that are no longer on the other side are gone. The sacks of dried fruits and vegetables are all but gone as well. The faeries that were with me said that they had an inventory sheet, and once we got that, we were more prepared to figure it out." Rocky looked at him before he continued. "I've had a lot of the things replaced already. As much as they could find. The trees, we're hoping, are stashed someplace else. Also, the foodstuffs are being taken to my mom's storage to dry for the stash here at the grounds. Lew has also been helping with some of the things that have been hard to come by today. He said that with his family they're around a great deal and have taken the faeries where he's spotted a few things. Such as plants and a few saplings that he's marked for future findings. I'm hoping that we can find where she's putting things."

"Why?" He said that he didn't see any reason for anyone to do without. "No. I'm sorry. I mean, why would she be stealing from her own foodstuffs? The seeds? Those are there for her, too. It's not as if she was paying for the things there. The trees? The same thing. And we've always had a system in place where if you were taking a lot of the supplies, you were to let someone know so that they could be replaced immediately. It's almost as if she—"

"That's what she's doing." Both he and Tellus looked at Rocky when she spoke up. "She's shorting your supplies to make you look incompetent. Not only that, but if she can do that, show you as being an unreliable queen, she has full rights to take over your realm and run it the way that—Christ, she's a great deal smarter than her father ever was. I'm not saying that I'm impressed, though I guess I am a little, but the fact that she has been thinking along these lines tells me that she's been reading up on all the books that are around about rules, too."

When Rocky stood up and began pacing, he looked at Tellus. She looked like she'd been hit between the eyes with something. He could almost feel sorry for her, but if she'd done more research on Holly before taking her on, then none of this would have happened. Mom appeared just as Tellus started to cry.

"You do that, and I'm going to smack you into next week. You need to get over this shit and do something about it. Stop waiting for the right moment. The right moment would have been not hiring her in the first place. But what is done is done. So, we move on from here. Where is she right now?" Tellus said that she was in her realm. "Good. We'll go there now and confront her. The other kings and queens are just waiting on word from you as to when we confront her as well. It seems as if a lot of your team has been abused sorely by her. Once we're all there, my son and his mate will come and save the day. Again. And if you so much as think that this is going to be blamed on anyone but yourself. I will leave you, Tellus. I've said this before, but I mean it more right now. I'll quit you. Our friendship, too."

"I don't want to do this anymore, Morgan." They held onto each other, and he decided that he needed to leave. Getting up, he was nearly to the cave when Rocky grabbed his hand and started pulling her along behind her.

"It's Holly." No one moved. The others showed up. Kings and queens that, while he knew of, he'd not ever met. "We have to go now."

They all appeared in a large yard. He didn't know what else to call it as it was devoid of everything but dirt and some bushes that looked like it had been dead for a while now. The castle wasn't in much better shape. There were pieces of it missing. One of the turrets had fallen in on the side of the castle and tore a gaping hole in the stone that was left open to the elements.

There were several trees around. He didn't know why they were still standing as they looked ready to fall over with a small breeze. Looking around, he could see that the entire area was devoid of anything that looked remotely like someone lived here who did landscaping. Or anything for that matter. There were no colorful flowers. Nothing was green. The castle, too, with all the damage that had been done to it, looked as if it had been abandoned decades ago.

"There she is." They watched Holly as she moved along the front of the castle. They all observed her tossing large stones into what he thought might have at one time been a waterway that supplied water to the landscaping. He wondered aloud if she had done anything at all to the place since her father had lived here. "How did you not see this, Tellus? When you visited her. How didn't you see the state of this place?"

"It never looked like this. And I was here mostly at night. But I would have noticed this lack of animals around along with their songs." He'd not noticed that, and now that he did, it caused him to shiver to know that it seemed as if the entire area was dead. "I'm going to let her see me. You all watch what happens. I'll call you when I need you."

As soon as Tellus called out, everything around the castle changed. The castle was bright with polished stones. The turret was back on the tall wall. Even the flowers and trees seemed to be fighting each other for the room around the place. It was redone so much that it made him ill to see so much done by magic.

"She's putting her off. I don't think she cares that Tellus showed up unannounced. Do you?" He told Mom that it didn't appear so. "You should shift, the two of you. I have a feeling that before this is finished, you're going to have to take the ground to the deepest point before it will be fixable. Then I think it will be a very long time before it will show even the slightest bit of beauty."

He thought his mom was right on that, too. Christ, he couldn't believe that they'd not noticed this before. He made his way with the others, slipping into the other realm just as Tellus was looking for them. Shiloh hadn't realized there had been a sort of veil around them, hiding them from not just the world beyond it but especially Holly when they entered the realm. It nauseated him to see her acting like a pleasant host. Even going as far as to invite them all in for freshly made tea and scones. He wouldn't eat or drink anything from this place for fear of being poisoned.

The rooms were devoid of much in the way of furniture. He was used to that. His mom told him once that castles were very large rooms, but they didn't need to be filled to the brim all the time. So when chairs began to appear, he leaned into Rocky and asked her if it was possible to see the room without all the glam.

"Of course." She touched her fingers to his forehead and then kissed him on the mouth. "The touch did it, but I needed a kiss from you. Look around. However, remember that you and I are the only ones seeing this. Unless your mom can, too. She's sneaky with her magic."

There were faeries bringing in the extra seating. They had been abused, too, the lot of them. As he watched them moving one heavy chair after the other, he realized that they were the ones holding the magic to the outside of the castle, too, so that he and the others could only see what Holly wanted them to. It occurred to him then that Holly wasn't using magic at all.

Did she not have any? Or did she have so very little that she couldn't make a simple thing like a room to have enough chairs in it? It bore thinking about. Then, why were the faeries beaten? Some of them were sporting black eyes. Broken limbs. Their wings, too, looked as if they'd been plucked at, with holes in them that would make it difficult to fly, much less move large pieces of furniture.

He put his hand out, and one of them came to sit on his palm. Putting the little woman up on his shoulder, he knew he was taking a chance here but was afraid if this was to come to a head today, and it looked like it was, then he wanted to get these little creatures out of here before they were killed. She poked him in his ear, and they had an immediate and profound connection. Shiloh asked the little person her name.

"Party, sir." He smiled and thought it might have been a good name for her a long time ago. *"You must be careful of the drinks here. They are poisoned with drugs that make it so you see only what she wants you to see. She knows of a witch that is doing this for her."*

He reached out to everyone in the room that he

had a connection with, including his mom, and told them what Party had said. He'd never seen so many cups hit their saucers at one time in his life. It was almost too funny. After telling Zippy and Veni the name of the witch, he let them take care of that.

"Where are the others? Surely, there are others like you that will need help getting out." Party told him that they were mostly dead. But there were a great many of them that had been pressed into service around this nasty castle. But most of them have been made into warriors who would only fight for her. *"I see. And can she do that? Have her own warriors?"*

"No, my lord. She cannot. It is written that she may have one, but she isn't to create one that would go against the queen that we all work for." He heard her moan a little, and he put up his finger for her to get healed. "Nay, sir. I shant be healed without the others. We all are suffering, and it wouldn't be fair of me to be well when there are so many of us who are in worse shape. I shall wait for you and your mate to free us all. That is what you're here to do, correct?"

"It is. We're all here to get Holly —"

"Shiloh, why aren't you having any of the tea that I've brewed. You have invaded my day —" Harsh laughter and then her saying that she was joking, then Holly spoke again. "I've so many new ideas that I want to talk to your mother and you about. The landscaping around your lands are in need of a good work-up. It's been years."

"I think our faeries take care of things pretty well. Mom too. You shouldn't waste your time on our land when it's doing so very well, Holly, and work on areas around here. It's looking a little barren, don't you think?" She asked him what he was talking about, a bit of her temper showing. He'd had enough of this woman. "When we arrived. I had a feeling then and more so now that you don't have any magic. You don't, do you? You've been relying on the faeries and other creatures to do your commands."

"I don't know what it is that you're talking about—is that one of my faeries on your shoulder there? Are you trying to steal from me, Shiloh? That's not nice at all. I'm going to have to insist that you release her before I get upset." Shiloh just crossed his arms over his chest and watched her. "Why are you here? All of you showing up at once. Why are you all here? I demand that you tell me and tell me the truth."

She had nothing. Not even enough magic to make him seriously think about telling her the truth.

When he looked around the room, everyone was staring at him and Holly. Her turning to them, too, pissed her off. Holly turned so sharply back toward him that he was a little startled himself.

"Get back to your tea, please. Not one of you has tasted even a bit of it." She looked back at him when it was apparent that something else occurred to her. "Ah, so you've been told of the magic, have you? Well, that's going to cost you, young Shiloh."

The room was suddenly filled with the buzzing of wings. Not just the kings and queens that were here by bequest of his mom, but there were thousands of fae and faerie alike hovering right above their heads with arrows pointed at each of the people in the room.

"Kill them. All of them save Roxanna. She's mine." No one moved. Not the fae nor faerie. Even Rocky seemed to be frozen. Holly ordered them to kill them all again. Then Rocky laughed.

"They can't do that. You should have known that, too. While I'm in charge, they'll listen to no one but me or Shiloh. The warriors, anyone volunteering or pressed into the service, only answer to us." She set her still-full cup of tea on the table. She faced the warriors in the room. "You will stand with her, and you will assuredly die. Or stand with me and have a much better chance of surviving this. Doing nothing will also get you killed. Which will it be?"

None of them moved. They were terrified. He could feel it like a thunderstorm coming across the open field. He had to do something. There was no reason for them to die today. Putting out his hand, he looked at the beaten warriors.

"You have been pressured into this service, haven't you?" Most of them nodded, their bows and arrows dropping down a bit. "You will not be punished by either of us nor the Queen Tellus if you drop your weapons and come with me now. We'll make sure that you're taken care of and that you're helped to get back up on your feet. There will be a job too if you wish it. Otherwise, you'll be taken care of for the rest of your life should you wish it. No harm needs to come to you today."

Several of the warriors began to speak at once. 'She's killed our mates, we have nothing left.' 'I have no one to care for me should I take your offer.' Others were saying how they were too beaten to do anything else. But he steadily held out his hand until one of the most beaten warriors fell into his palm.

"It's too late for most of us, my lord. Please

make sure that you take care that our families are well cared for. We—"

"Oh, for the love of it all. Just kill it. I'm sick of its whining." Shiloh snatched his hand back before Holly could crush the fae in his hand. "You're nothing, Shiloh. The same as Rocky here. She killed my father, and now she will have to pay for his death. I had a better plan, I will admit that, but you and that fucking bitch messed things up for me, and now I'm pissed off. Warriors, kill them or die."

All the weapons hit the floor. It was a tinkling sound, much like small bells. But its meaning was much harsher. They all were telling Holly that they didn't want to be her warriors. Not only that, when they moved en mass out of the castle, the rooms took on the appearance of what it really looked like.

"Be gone." He'd forgotten about the others in the room. When Tellus pointed her magic at Holly, her scream of pain was abruptly cut off. She was dead. And the castle somehow knew it. It began to fall in and crumble as if it, too, had been pressed into service that it no longer wanted to do. They all raced out of the building. Picking up the small wounded creatures, he put them all along his body as he shifted. Being as large as he could, he was able too to be able to knock out some of the stones that dropped at the entrance of the place before trapping them inside.

As he burst through the castle wall, he scooped up three of the kings with their mates. He saw, just out of the corner of his eye, that Rocky was doing the same. Picking people up and literally tossing them out of the hole he'd made. By the time the castle was down completely, he'd made two more trips inside and brought out all the beings inside with the help of his own mate.

The dust was still settling around the ruined walls of the castle when he set the faeries and fae alike along the tree line so that they'd be safe. Mom called for the faeries from the castle that Tellus had, and they began working on the injured. It wasn't until later that he realized that Tellus was nowhere to be seen. Shiloh asked his mom where she was.

"She's gone back to her castle. Which is where she needs to be. There will be plenty of questions for her to answer." He nodded. "For now, we'll take care of the people here. That's all we can do. Tellus is being queen. That's what the people need. To see that no matter what happened here or any place, she is the one in charge. As it should be."

He worked to keep water and sugar for the

hurt by having others run to retrieve as much as they could from the fresh fruit on his family's land. He'd already had several glasses of the cool liquid himself and felt so much better for it. He also made sure that Rocky and his mom did as well. When the others showed up, they, too, helped out. They all thought it would be some time before this area was ever a good place to be.

Chapter 5

They worked tirelessly for a month on the land. Rocky had had Shiloh dig great trenches in the earth once the land was clear of the stones and other debris they'd discovered around the nearly dead land. She was so happy that Shiloh had worked with the faeries who had been at Holly's beck and call to get things cleaned up. It made them feel like they were now being productive, and that was a good feeling for them all.

"Once the land is opened up, we should be able to have Tellus bring in the rains to give the grounds a good soaking." Rocky told Morgan that she thought that would be the best thing for it. "It hurts me so much to see this like it is. If we can just get a couple of trees planted and a few shrubs, I would feel so much better."

"It'll be a while, I'm thinking. The faeries are

too worn out to bring in much in the way of magic." They both looked up when the sky darkened. Rocky thought that it was Tellus bringing in the rains already. "What the hell is that?"

The sky began to brighten as the swarm of small creatures began to land on the earth. Most of them were fae, but there were also brownies and faeries too. They were all loaded down with something, and when she made her way to them, she realized that they were from all around the world. Most of them, she realized, too, were warriors who had their bows and arrows still upon their backs.

"My lady." She asked the one that came forward what was going on. "Your mate called out to any that could come and help here. He said there was a lot to be done, but we needed to work together to get this place back in shape. It was difficult not to have everyone come to his call. It's wonderful to be needed for such a worthy cause."

Just then, Shiloh showed up. He kissed her on the mouth and told her what his plan was. The fae, his name was Butch, said that they'd done what Shiloh had wanted and brought more arrows than they would use in war. She asked him what his plan was.

As the days had gone on, it was apparent to her that Shiloh had a deeper connection to the earth than she did. Not only that, but he'd brought in Sammy, the king of gnomes, to advise on things that were going on. Today, after working so hard, he thought it was time that they could plant some seeds, though deeper than they normally would in the earth, and then have it watered for several days. The earth was much too dry for it to harm to be watered so much, and she thought it a splendid idea.

It took him only a few minutes to line up his plan. The warriors would hover above the land with their arrows dipped in his blood. Then, while still moist, a seed would be put to the tip of the arrow and shot, as deeply as they could, into the still-wet earth.

It wasn't just flowers that would be planted but whatever they had in the way of seeds. Trees and plain shrubs would be planted later, but for now, they were planting foodstuff, flowers, flowering shrubs, as well as bushes with berries. After the first section of the earth was planted, they made a few adjustments and moved to the second section. As far as Rocky could see, it was working out very well.

By the time that Tellus started the rain, the

land was planted. She was so excited that Shiloh had made this work that she wanted to hug him to pieces as the land and the surrounding area began to sprout, just a few sprouts of the tiny seeds that had been planted. But she had to ask him why he'd had the arrows dipped in his blood.

"I'm one with the earth, as are you. So I thought that with that magic, it wouldn't hurt to have a little bit of extra going into the ground with the seeds. If it works, great. If not, I'm not really out that much. But it looks like it might well have helped, don't you think?" She nodded, so happy with the starting results. "I just heard from the faeries that I sent out last week. They've found the trees. However, they've been destroyed for the most part. They were able to find a few seeds but not nearly as many of the trees that she killed."

"I'm so sorry to hear that." He said that he was, as well. "Some good news is that Lew and part of his harem have found some of the missing trees on your mom's land. Not just a few, either. They were in the deepest part of the land, more than likely the reason that they were thought to be all gone. As it is now, I'm having the faeries mark them so that when the time is right, they can be moved without anything harming them."

He kissed her again, and she smiled up at him. "Two things too that you should know. The castle is going to be built by Veni and Zippy. It will perpetually be held with magic. As the years go on, whoever is there will be able to have all the latest magic to keep it in good shape. Internet, which I guess they're trying to get Tellus to use, as well as cable, should they just want to chill and watch a movie or something. Second thing. And this isn't really important, but it is good that you should know. The stones that were left here when the castle collapsed are going to be left here as a reminder of what happens to idiots who think they can take over the realm. There is also going to be a sign made so that anyone who comes around will be required to read it. And, I almost forgot, there is now going to be a calendar of events going out, like special plantings or things like that. Mom is also going to be putting out something that will tell anyone who wants to know that she has extra of things that she's planted. I think that will be a big hit, though mom doesn't think that anyone will care if she has too many pumpkins or tomatoes."

"Has your mom always undervalued herself like that?" Shiloh said that she had since he'd been a child. "I don't want to point out how long that's been and that she should be over it, but we'll move on. All right. We have plans in the works, and I, for one, am thrilled beyond words that it's happening."

Rocky just wanted to go home, put her feet up, and rest. It had been a grueling few weeks, and she was about as exhausted as she'd ever been. The good news was that she'd been handed all the books that Tellus had collected from Holly's underground lair and had been put in charge of making sure that they were safe. Where she'd gotten them—or where her father had gotten them too wasn't anything that she was going to think about. They were safe, and that's what mattered.

By the time the sun was coming up, she was finally home. When she arrived in their bedroom, Shiloh had set up a deep tub of hot water for her to soak in, little sandwiches that she could nibble on, as well as glasses of juice. She was nearly asleep when she finally got out of the still-warm tub and into bed. Christ, she felt fantastic.

It was still dark out when she woke. While she had an idea that she'd slept around the clock, she didn't know for sure. Getting up, she staggered her way to the bathroom and took a long hot shower.

As she was getting out, drying off with the most amazingly fluffy towel, she thought of Shiloh and reached out to him. It made her feel terrible that she'd not thought of him as soon as her eyes opened, and she was glad when he spoke to her with a happy-sounding voice.

"I'm at the castle. I'm not sure what anyone is going to call it, but for now, I'm just calling it a castle. Anyway, it worked. The flowers, thanks to all the water and the attendance of the little creatures, are all in bloom. Not only that but there seem to be enough flowers around that Tellus had gone to make sure that some of them, well, most, I guess, are going to have faeries drop." She asked him if she was happy with the progress. "Oh yes. She's been doing a little dance every few feet. I think her happiness is spreading as the other creatures around, and there are a great many of them now who are happy as well. I've been told no less than a dozen times that with her happiness means that there will be an abundance of newborns born here, too. Of every creature that is here. Lew is out of his mind with happiness as well."

"I'd forgotten about that. That's good, too. With all the death that has been discovered, it's good to know that the next generation is being born. How does the castle look? I'm assuming that I missed it being made." Shiloh told her that she had needed the rest, and yes, it was up. "Good. I'm so happy to hear that. I'll have to talk to Zippy and Veri about their help with it. It's wonderful how your family can be depended on when they're needed."

"You're a part of that, too, my dear heart." He laughed a little. "You didn't ask, but I'll tell you. Yes, that means that you will be having a baby too with all the time you spent here. And anyone that hadn't been breeding before of my family, they are now. It's a wonderful thing, don't you think?"

"I do." Rocky put her hand over her flat belly. "A baby. We didn't talk about that too much. I'm assuming that you're all right with that."

"I couldn't be happier if you are. I am looking forward to seeing you heavy with our baby. Not only that, but seeing them running around the land and having fun. Just thinking of a baby makes me all mushy inside." She called him a goof. "Yes, I guess that I am. But I'm your goof, so that makes it just fine."

She agreed. When she was ready to leave the house, she made sure that there was nothing going on that she needed to be aware of. Dinner was going to be a few sandwiches, but tomorrow night, it would be comfort food. Her favorite meal. She didn't even care what it was, but having it at home with the two of them was more than she could have hoped for.

She couldn't believe the improvement that two days had made — she had slept through the day, twice as it turned out, but felt better for it. There were flowers with long stems that were heavy with dew. Bushes were so full of berries and other fruits that she was sure that they'd be enough to save seeds for the next planting. Even the few trees that had been planted because Shiloh said that it wouldn't hurt to test were full of leaves and as strong as anything that she'd ever seen.

"Oh, it's so lovely." She was dancing around, too, when it occurred to her that she had nearly stepped on a few plants. But it mattered little to the people there. Everyone was in such a good mood. "Just look at all this. Other lands will want the same treatment if word gets around about how much of a change things are going on around here."

"I hope so." She hugged Tellus and was surprised when she had. "Don't stop doing that. I think that it made my heart a bit lighter knowing that you're just as happy as I am right now. Just look at all this, Rocky. That mate of yours, he'd been directing everyone in the right direction for hours, and no one seemed the least bit unhappy about it. My goodness, even the trolls are being so helpful. And Shiloh has made sure that they're getting some of the fruits for their labor as well. Did he tell you that he's planted a garden out behind the new castle? Oh, don't get me started on the castle. Oh, it's so lovely on the inside. There's a drying room that is already filled to the brim with things grown right here. The seeds that had been missing are all but stocked up again. And the trees? Well, let me just tell you that with all the help, we've been able to locate so many more than we had before that we'll be planting things for generations from now on."

The two of them toured the area. She could see bits of the things that Shiloh had made happen. There was a large resting area that had been set up with fresh fruits and vegetables. Not only was there plenty of juice to be had, but fresh spring water that was icy cold, too. And shade. The trees that had been planted were being used as a cover from the warm sun and keeping people happy.

"I love it all. I'm not normally so mushy about things, but this really does get my heart feeling so full." Tellus and Morgan, who had joined them in the garden area, agreed with her. "Don't get used to me being nice. Tomorrow I'll be right back to my bitchy self. Oh, I can't believe how much has been accomplished."

"I'm so glad that you're happy with it all. I knew that you were coming and was so nervous about what you'd think." She asked Tellus why she'd care about her opinion. "You're going to have to pick the next landscaper. I've decided that I'm not cut out for the job. Morgan said that you'd do it so that the next person would be perfect for the role. I believe her. I also think that you might well know who needs to be in place and should have been all along."

"I do." She looked at Morgan. "You have to help me convince him that he'd be perfect for the job. Shiloh has done this without any thought that he'd not be in charge later down the line. I can't think of a better, more qualified person for the job, can you?"

"No. But what about him being there for you? Or, for that matter, being there on the leap with us? I don't want to have to travel all the way here to see my baby boy or any children that the two of you have." Rocky said that she'd have her own entrance to their land, but it didn't have to work like that. He wouldn't have to be as hands-on with the things that he'd put in place so that communication was better than ever. "You're thinking that he'll be able to be on the leap and walk away from this daily?"

"I do. For the simple reason that he's very good at this." They all three looked around. "He's got it set up so that the next person, him, I'm hoping, will only need to keep an eye on things rather than to have to make it work daily. I noticed the planting schedule that he's made. The way that he's put in places where new landscaping will need to be done. He also has reminders that he'll send out when something comes up that needs immediate care. And if you think about it, there is little of that needed nowadays. He's got it so there is an eye on everything."

"Yes, you're right about that. He's magically set up cameras on places that are in need of some work, as well as places that it looks like he's been given a heads up about that will change. It never occurred to me that we were missing so much without direct communication about landslides, water damage, and the like. This way, he has an eye on all of it." Rocky mentioned, too, that their children would be brought up to know how to work the magic, too, so that it could be handed down to each generation without missing a beat. "I love that idea as well. Perhaps it would save a great deal of time to just have all areas handed down by generation after generation from now on. I know that I'd be happy not to have to pick someone to do the job."

As it turned out, it didn't take any convincing at all to have Shiloh take over the job. He was also going to be able to make sure that the kingdom was safe for Tellus and them as well. The castle was going to be a sort of hub, a place to go when there was an issue. Though Rocky didn't think there was going to be too much of that going around now either. Things weren't perfect, but they were about as close as they could be. And she couldn't have been prouder in that moment than if she'd come up with the ideas that Shiloh had. He was a brilliant, loving man. And he was all hers.

~*~

Shiloh held the baby to his shoulder when she'd finished with her bottle. Today had been a celebration for the earth, and he was so happy with the turnout. He had been going between the buffet table and the guests for the last two hours, and he was tired. But when someone shoved a baby — quite literally — into his arms, he was content to sit and hold her.

"She's a cutie. Do you know who she belongs to?" He laughed as he handed the baby over to his older brother, Carroll. "Look at all those curls, Shiloh. She looks like a pixie. Mom would be over the moon if any of us were to have a redheaded little girl. And the curls would be a bonus."

"I think that mom is thinking of kidnapping her." They both laughed, but Carroll quieted down when he startled the little girl awake. "I believe her name is Frida. Her twin, a little brother, is with his grandma. Apparently, Grandma isn't too keen on the fact that she's a redhead. While I guess I get that some people believe all the hype about redheads being evil, I don't. But Freddie isn't a redhead and doesn't have a single freckle on his little face."

"That's just stupid." He thought that as well but just watched his brother rock the little girl. "Did you know that Frida means peace? I just thought of that. Perhaps they named her that in hopes of it having an effect on their grandma. If it doesn't, then it's her loss." Carroll looked at the little girl. "You ever need some grandma-loving, little girl, you just call out to my momma. She'll love you to bits."

Kissing the little girl on her forehead, he handed her back to him. Putting her up on his shoulder, he asked his brother what was going on. When he didn't answer him right away, he waited. That was the thing about his brother that he loved. When he had something to say to you, you could bet that he'd worked it all out in his head.

"I'm thinking that we're going to need more land before too much longer. I know that mom has a lot of investments that she is to use as they come up, but we're using the land up faster than I think anyone realized." He asked him what he meant. "We're putting in a new orchard. I think you knew that. Until the land is cleared of the older trees and transplants are made, there is very little room for the gardens to take hold where the old orchard was. I don't even think that we're waiting nearly long enough to give the land some rest before we begin on that project. We've had an orchard there for decades. The land is tired and worn out as I've ever seen it."

"All right. I understand the concerns, but other than just taking the trees out and letting them lay by, what do you suggest? I'm assuming you have an idea how this will work." Carroll said that he didn't, actually. "That's surprising. I would have thought that you'd have a failproof plan all worked out."

"You don't have to be nasty about it." He

assured his brother that he wasn't. But that he sincerely believed that he'd have a plan. "I'm sorry. I'm just worried, that's all. I don't want anything to go unplanned."

"All right. Let me think a moment." And he did. Thinking about the massive size of the new orchard plans as compared to the older one. There was a lot of size difference. But he didn't think that was what Carroll was talking about. "Okay, so you're worried about the amount of land. Or is it the trees that will be set aside?"

"Both." Shiloh nodded. "Mom said that she'd be all right with not having an orchard for a few years. I don't know that she's really thought about how much we do with the trees and the families around town right now. To not have trees, even for a season, will be hard on a lot of people that have come to depend on the fruits."

"I think that mom might be right. Have you been to the storage shed where she keeps fruits in? I think that if we were to give each and every family a bushel of fruit for the next three years, there would be a great deal still left over. In addition to that, she has enough frozen or canned too that we could supply them with the fixings for pies and jams too."

Carroll said that wasn't fresh. "No. But it is good. And if you're really worried about the amount of land that we're using up, think about all the land that hasn't been touched in years that is out in the pastures where we put the meat that we use for ourselves. Just a couple of weeks ago, I heard Mom say that we don't need any fresh on-the-hoof meat for a while until we use up some of the things that she has smoked or just put up. We've been through that before. Cutting back on the meat or simply giving a cow or two to those that want it that live in town. I think that's worked out well for a lot of people."

"That's true. I'd forgotten about that." He still didn't look convinced. "What about the land that we need to put the cattle on if we've planted it full of trees? Then what do we do?"

He smacked his brother on the shoulder. When he asked him what that was for, Shiloh looked at Frida, who was staring at him. Smiling, he calmly told her why he'd smacked his big brother.

"Because he's a big dummy, dumbhead. That is making himself stressed about things that will work themselves out on their own. So what if we plant the pastures full of trees. The natural fertilizer will be good for them. The ground will get a good working over, and the fruit will be extra wonderful for it all. As for where we put the cows and other animals? Well, we didn't plant the land where the trees were supposed to go in the first place, now did we." He kissed the little girl on the head before turning to his brother. "I know for a fact that the land earmarked for the new orchard isn't set in stone. And if Mom heard you worrying about it, she'd hit you harder than I did. What's really up your butt today?"

"I don't have anything to do." Just as he was ready to smack him again, he put up his hands to stop him. "You have the landscaping job. The others all have shit to do that gets their blood moving in the morning. I have things, too, but nothing as important as what you five are doing. And if I bring this up to Hanna again, I swear to you she's going to leave me. I'm driving her insane. I wanted you to tell me that I was to work on it right away and not stop until it was perfect. Or as perfect as I could get it. But you have it all worked out, and you've not even left the chair you're sitting in."

He looked at his brother for a full minute before he handed him the baby again. When he just sat there, staring off into space, thinking of the best way to knock some sense into his head, Rocky came and sat on the ground in front of him. Without saying a word, she took his hand into hers and stared at Carroll. He looked like he was getting uncomfortable with her staring, too.

"Let me get this straight. You're whining that you have nothing important going on when you're the head of this family. Not only that, but to me, and I want you to understand that I'd rather kill you than to be nice to you — you have one of the most important jobs of any of us. You keep us in money. Not that we're going to run out of it anytime soon, but there is no point in letting that go until we're close; now, is there?" He said that all he had to do was invest daily. "Then what do you do? Sit around whining at home to Hanna about how much you don't have to do?"

"No. Well, I did, but she put a stop to that, too." Rocky told him that it was better her than if she did it. "Yeah, she told me that too. That if anyone heard me whining, which I want to point out that I wasn't, then I'd be talking out of the other side of my head. I don't understand how that is supposed to work, but I think she meant business."

"Of course she did. And so do I. All right. You want an important job to do. I think that the one that you're doing right now is pretty fucking important.

The mother of these twins is having a rough time. Did you know that her husband was in a car accident about a week ago? She's not had a moment's peace with his family coming around all the time 'helping' her. They don't do anything remotely helpful, but they're there, stuck up her ass and making comments about how when he lived at home with them, he wasn't in any car accident then. Liars. He had four of them when he lived at home, but they're not remembering that while they make poor Lynda cry all the time. You're giving her a much-needed break. And when I get up from here after I find you a fucking binkie, I'm going to go get her son and hold him for a little while as I send her into the castle to have a long, much-needed nap." She looked at him before continuing to Carroll. "Also, you want to help? Keep your nose around town in being able to be aware of what is happening with people like her husband. She could use not just a break but someone to help her with groceries. A check for help with the bills — which are higher thanks to his family sponging off her. Also, get them out of the fucking house. Hire her a staff. She can't afford it usually, but it would be nice for her to get some rest before her husband comes home to a nearly keeled-over wife, don't you think?"

"Are there many people around town that are like her? Needing help?" Rocky handed Carroll a sheet of paper. "Christ, so many names. Why hasn't anyone said anything to me before now?" She only cocked a brow at Carroll, and he seemed to understand. "Because I've been a pain in the ass and whiny about shit without doing anything about it. All right. I got it. I'm going to work on this now."

"Don't overwhelm people with your help, Carroll. No one will appreciate you being too helpful for them. When they say they could use some help with groceries, they only mean a gift card or two. Not for you to go out and buy out the store for them. If they tell you that they need a ride to and from the doctor, don't be buying them a car. That's not what they said. Listen to them. With your ears, not your head. They don't expect it all to be — well, some will, but most people don't expect you to give them everything at once." Carroll told him he might well have done that, too. "Of course, you would have. You have a big heart. And I couldn't love you any more than I do right now for thinking that way. But in moderation. Just a little help at a time will go a long way in keeping us not only in money of our own but enough to help out the town when it's needed."

Carroll, armed with his list after handing the little girl to Rocky, walked away. He did seem to have a lighter step as he moved across the lawn, and Shiloh was glad for it. Rocky said his name, and he looked at her with a smile.

"You're a good sister-in-law. Did you know that?" She asked him why he'd say that. "Because I know for a fact that you've had that list for a couple of days. And I'm sure that if I were to look it over, I'd also see the roofs that need to be replaced as well as the grounds on it. He'll be busy for a while now with that." She said that Hanna had talked to her about it. "I'm sure that she had plenty to say too. Do you have more lists that are going to be handed out when the other wives send their whining mates to you? I know for a fact that Bailey is in trouble with Zippy. And that just the other day, Scout was bitching about how he'd been kicked out of the house when he'd gotten in Allison's way when she was making pies for the food drive."

"I do, as a matter of fact. None for you. I think that you have enough on your plate right now with the new landscaping job. However, I can see you getting in early on working, making a list of what you want done, and being home for dinner every evening, too. You're not the type of person to put things off." He said that he'd never been that way. "I didn't think so. I'm glad for that. How about we go and get Freddie and take both him and his sister for a walk. I wasn't kidding when I said that I'd sent their mother to the castle for a much-needed nap. Not from them but from her in-laws. Why is it that some in-laws think that their child is the perfect spouse in the family, and all the trouble lies directly at the feet of the other half? I'm so glad your mom isn't like that. She thinks I'm more perfect than you are."

"Really?" They did get the little boy and take their walk. It was something that he enjoyed more than anything, just taking a walk and seeing what needed to be done or was being worked on. Shiloh thought that a lot of trouble brewing could be taken care of if they just took a walk in a forest together. It was calming in ways that no one could imagine.

The Future

Shiloh could see his granddaughter sitting in the sun with her body swaying to the trees. It was a method that all of them used when they were stressed, taught to them by the previous king of Gnomes, Thad. Now that Sammy was in charge of them, he had all of the animals on the land using the same method to relax and chill out. However, it hadn't been working for Albry.

He noticed his mom standing there with a freshly dried towel to her face. She'd been out hanging those same towels when he'd brought Albry over this morning. Something had to be done. Someone, him, he thought, needed to talk to his youngest grandchild.

Sitting next to the tree where she was, he watched his mom gather up her clean laundry and head into the house. Mom had wanted Albry to come over today. She thought that they could do things together, and it would bring her out of this shell she was in. Apparently, it hadn't worked. But when Albry leaned her back against his shoulder, he took that as a good sign.

"Everyone is worried about you. I'm sure you know that." Instead of answering him, she reached for his hand and cradled it in her lap. "I love you, Albry. I love you very much. I hope you also know that everyone here loves—"

"Thomas Moore was a good person." He closed his mouth and waited for her to hopefully continue. "So was his sister, Gladys. They no more decided this on their own than I did to have to kill them. It was them or me."

"I understand." This time, he squeezed her hand. "You can tell me, honey. I'll make sure that the police know. But there has to be some explanations about what went down there. There are just too many deaths for someone not to have to be charged with this."

Albry was twelve, almost thirteen this year. She had three older brothers who she'd been wrestling with since she'd been in diapers. Albry and he, her dad being his grandson, Spencer from his oldest son,

Milo, had formed a special bond like none of the other children that had been born in his family. From the moment that she looked up at him, just being born, he knew that she was going to be just like him. A faerie cat with wings.

"I didn't want to go to the mall with them. I know you heard that. Because I wanted to hang out here with Grandma Morgan. It was jelly-making day." He smiled a little but didn't interrupt her. "I'm not saying that I still wished I had stayed home. I know that it was because of me that more people weren't killed, but I don't think that's a good enough reason to have to go shopping. Who wants to hang out at a stupid mall when there is all this around here to take up your time?"

"No. I have to agree with you there. But even Grandma told you that you need to hang out with people more your own age, honey. You hang out with all these adults, and you might be old before your time." She snorted at him, and Shiloh laughed. "But you were there, and you did save those people. Even after killing the two of them, you still managed to get everyone out of the building by pulling the fire alarm. The place had been rigged to go up, as you know." She leaned her head on his shoulder, turning enough so they were facing the same way. "What made you be alerted to the trouble?"

"Gladys said something to me the other day. How she and her brother had big plans for the mall. Then she told me not to go. That…she said that if I happen to go, then it would all be on me." She turned and looked at him. "I didn't even think about that until just this minute. She warned me away. So I'd not get hurt."

He thought it was more than likely due to the fact that Albry had special powers and that she'd spoil their plans if she were to show up. But she had, and he couldn't have been happier with the outcome. Especially since she was talking about it now.

"The girls and I were in the food court. I was having a malt while the rest of them were having cinnamon rolls. Even though I don't gain weight, I can't stand all that sugar that they put on them. Then, there is the dipping sauce that you're supposed to use. Yuck. Nothing but sugar and water if you ask me." He didn't ask her to remain on track with her tale. He knew better than most that getting some of the other things out there made the problem or issue seem less harsh. More like it was just a normal day for her. And Shiloh loved her for that. "The new candy store was just two shops down. I was going to get some of the lemon drops for you and my dad. He loves them as much as you do."

"My mom could never get them to harden when she made them. They did, however, make the best lemon syrup to pour over ice cream in the world. But you're right. Your dad loves them as much as I do." He watched the trees swaying as he continued. "Next spring, we'll have plenty of syrup to go around to all of us."

They were quiet, the two of them. He had never been one to fill out the empty spaces, and neither had Albry. Her mom was a chatterbox. They all loved Laura to pieces, but she couldn't stand the quiet. It was just something that they all had gotten used to, he supposed.

"Thomas killed three people in the candy store before I could stop him. I guess he killed more than that as he made his way into the mall, but I'd been inside and didn't hear what was going on." He waited, holding his breath for what she was going to tell him next. "When he came into the mall, he was at the other end from me. But I could feel the panic of all those around us. He had been firing randomly at people and killing them. Gladys had, I guess, gone to the second floor. She had been firing at people from that level that were below her. She and Thomas had already killed eighteen people before I could stop them."

The way that she was describing what was going on, he could see it in her mind. She and the girls that she'd been with had been sitting at the food court complaining about the homework that they had to do all summer. He could see too that Albry had already read the required books the previous year, but she didn't comment. As brilliant as she was, she tended to hide her intelligence under her hat, so to speak, so she'd not be teased. He knew the exact moment that Albry heard the first of many more gunshots.

"What was that?" Albry had warned the others to stay put while she had a look. "No. You're going to get more candy than us. We'll go with—"

"That's a gunshot sound." The other girls, ready to leap on Albry, had turned to the blonde that was with them. "I know that sound. Someone is shooting in the mall, and we need to hide."

"Get out. And tell as many people as you can to get out, too. I don't know...pull a fire alarm." The blonde told the others she'd do that, but they were complaining about how illegal it was to pull a fire alarm when there wasn't a fire. "There is also a law about shooting people, too. Would you rather be dead or in trouble? I'm thinking I'd rather be alive."

The shot that took out the blonde girl made the others stand there like they were ready to be hit next. Instead of letting them get killed, Albry had shoved them to get moving, and they started screaming as they made their way to the exit, right in line of fire to Thomas.

Two more of her friends were shot but would live. One of them had complained that with her being shoved by Albry, she'd broken her wrist when she fell. The man interviewing her later would ask her if she would rather have joined her friend in death or to nurse a broken arm. The child said that it was coming up on prom season, and she didn't want to have to wear a cast. Albry hadn't gone to see any of the other girls either since that day. It was doubtful to him that Albry was going to be missing their kind of friendship.

"Gladys saw me about the time I had gotten the girls I was with to start moving. She fired twice at me. I remember thinking at the time that she was a good shot with that rifle. It was as big as anything that I'd ever seen." Albry looked up at him. "Thank you, Grandpa Shiloh. I'm feeling better with the more of it I tell you."

"You tell me as much as you can. I'll relay it to the police. I think you're parents will be happy too to find out that you've decided to talk about that day." She said she didn't know if he was going to be happy when she got to the end. "I'll be here for you, baby girl. And what you're telling me can't hurt you anymore. It's done. You're only telling the story now. Nothing can hurt you from a tale. Remember that."

"I do." She, as he had done, drank a bit of the juice that some of the faeries had brought. Sitting his glass to the side, he waited for her to continue. He didn't have long to wait.

"I came up on Gladys first. She was holding her foot on the neck of Officer Pantalette while she reloaded her gun. I saw then that she had two more weapons on her. A couple of knives, too. When she bent over to pick up a shell for the shotgun she'd brought, I tackled her from behind and broke her neck." Shiloh closed his eyes. That had been one of the questions that had come from the police. Who had killed Gladys? Since he knew now, he had to come up with a plausible story that people around the world would be able to believe. An adrenal rush was all he could think of on how his tiny granddaughter had broken the neck of a girl as tall and heavy as Gladys had been.

"It took me a long time to find Thomas. I didn't know that he was on the lower level until I saw him from the upper one. There was a trail of bodies behind him as he made his way to the center of the mall. That was where most of the people were gathered. I don't know why they thought that was a good hiding place, but they were like those games where he shoots one, and the next one pops up. When I caught up with him, there were fourteen of them already dead."

Forty-seven people had been murdered that day at the mall. Six more from their home, including their four brothers, sister, and father. The two teenagers, both older than Albry, had come prepared to kill a great many more. Even if you didn't count the explosives that they'd planted in the mall the week before, they were going to kill everyone they came across. Reaching for Albry, he held her tightly to his chest as she continued.

"Thomas asked me to join him in the fun. That's what he called it: fun. I declined, telling him that he had to stop. But when he laughed, I knew that he wasn't going to. Not only that, but I think he was fully prepared to kill me, too." She sniffled, and he handed her a handkerchief from his pocket. "You always said that to have a clean hanky for a girl in distress was the sign of a true gentleman. Thank you, Grandpa Shiloh."

"You're so very welcome, love. You tell me the rest, and we'll sort this out with the police. You're not in trouble, never that. But the sooner we can get you better and this behind us, the better the town will be as well." She nodded and held tightly to the hanky he'd given her. Shiloh couldn't imagine the horrific things that she'd seen that day other than looking in her mind.

~*~

Albry waited for the police to speak again. She'd agreed to come here with her grandpa Shiloh when she woke up. After talking to him yesterday morning, she'd gone to bed and had slept all through the day and into the night. She thought it was the first real rest she'd had since this thing had started. Albry thought of herself as the luckiest girl in the world.

"So you said you came up on Thomas, and he asked you to join him. Did he say what he wanted you to join him in?" She said that he'd not explained, but she assumed it was in killing people as he'd kicked a gun in her direction. "There had to be a reason that he thought that he could have trusted you not to use the gun that he'd only just given you. Why would he think that?"

"It wasn't loaded. When I picked it up from the floor and fired it at him, I figured out it was empty." That's all she said. She'd been schooled on what to answer and what to ignore, or she'd be all fuzzier up with what had happened. The next officer asked her how she'd figured that out. "Well, since I was aiming at his head and he didn't fall back, I just assumed it was empty. Then I opened the magazine up and didn't see any ammo in it."

Two of the officers laughed but quickly turned it into a cough. She didn't understand how that was supposed to work in not knowing it was laughter, but she didn't care. After talking to her grandpa, Shiloh, she felt like she could take on the police station here. Grandpa had told her that they didn't think she'd done anything wrong. They were just as scared as she'd been while things were going to shit. These were things that none of them had encountered ever before.

After telling them how she'd killed Thomas

again—by ripping his throat out as her cat, she was told that she could go home. There was more to that story, to all the story that had happened that day. But Grandpa Shiloh told her that the meat and potatoes of it was all they wanted. The details, or the gravy, were just too much for them. They wanted a settled case, not to have nightmares for the rest of their lives.

Not that she had nightmares about what she'd done. Grandma Morgan had told her that she had saved not just the people in the mall that day, which was a wonderful thing, but she had also saved two presidents, five doctors, and a woman who would go on to cure cancer by the people not dying. The silver lining of saving them, she told her.

Albry met up with her grannie Morgan at her shop when she's been freed. Going into the shop, she knew just where she'd be and went to hug her. They stood that way, holding onto each other tightly for a good ten minutes. It was more than she could have hoped for and better than anything that she could have imagined.

"Are you finished with this nonsense?" She told her what the officer told her. "Not to leave town? Where did he expect you to go when you're just a child and have no way of learning to drive. My goodness, the things that people say when they're upset. Are you hungry? I have some pies just coming out of the oven."

The two of them sat in the back of the bakery and had two slices of her pies each. The faeries were decorating cupcakes to be sold, and she snatched herself one of those too. She loved the faeries and wouldn't know what to do without one by her side all the time. After taking some sugared flowers from the small tin of them on the table, she laid them out some water, too, to drink while she sat there.

"Next week, we have those chicks coming in. I was hoping you'd be around to help me put up the pens tomorrow." She said that she'd be happy to help. "Good. I thought you'd say that. My daughter is coming home, too, tomorrow. I'm not sure how I feel about that. She'll want to fuss at me."

"Smack her around then. I know that you want to when she tries that crap with you." Albry turned then to look at her Grannie Morgan. "I love you, Grannie. So much. I know that I scared you a bit, and I'm sorry for that. But…well, I'd never killed anyone before, and I didn't know that it would make me feel so bad when I had to do it. Why did it hurt me so badly that I had to kill Gladys and Thomas? They weren't good people."

"No. But you are, and that's what bothers you. Not only did you not want them to die, even though that is where it ended, you shouldn't have had to be in that position in the first place. My heart hurts that you had to witness that and to fix things there. However, I'm so very proud of you for getting your ass in gear and getting things done." She thought about what her grannie had said and agreed with her. When she returned, she asked her why Molly was coming home. "She has it in her head that I'm much too old to be working around here anymore. She wants to take me to her town and show me what I'm missing. That girl. I swear to you, I think that she was switched at birth with my real daughter. But I love her to pieces. Her and her sisters."

Grannie Morgan had had five daughters when she married Grandpa. He had three children from his previous marriage and had blended well with the others who lived around here. But Grannie's youngest had been the odd man, or she supposed the odd woman out. She wasn't horrible or anything like that. Aunt Molly was funny and easy to talk to. She just did not like the leap. Nor any of the animals that had come with it.

Molly had gone to college and had never returned. She had found herself a mate and had brought him home to meet the family. But he, like Molly, didn't like the farm life. He didn't even care for the fresh taste of the things that had been grown here to eat. Albry thought it was funny. That for centuries and centuries, Grannie and her family had lived here, and only one person out of all those born and raised here had left. It showed Albry that Grannie Morgan was the best there was at being head of the family.

The two of them were just finishing up the chicken coop as the chicks had arrived early when she said she'd had enough for the day. The two of them made dinner for them and Grandda when he got home. She loved her grandda, but she had to admit that her Grandpa Shiloh was her favorite. He never had too much to do to explain things to her, and when he did explain things, he would also have her work on the question so that she'd know it physically as well. Grandda was much too busy bringing in the crops. Whatever that meant.

She thought that he just didn't care for little girls. Whatever his reason, Grandpa Shiloh had made up for it in keeping her happy. She so loved her family.

All of her uncles, Grannie Morgan's boys, she called them, were the best that there was. She could just sit quietly in a chair and listen to them tell stories about their life growing up here for days if she could. They were all smart, too. Each of them had gone to college several times, just as she planned to do, and were good at all kinds of things. But it was Grannie Morgan that she was most proud to call Grannie.

While she'd only been a child, her parents had plotted to have her killed. Then, after that was settled, she became one of the most influential women in the world. But she didn't leave her little area to do talks as everyone wanted her to do—the smells in bigger cities were making her ill so much that she'd have to rest up for days afterwards. But she did write books. Even illustrated the pictures that she needed to make things work around other farms trying to do what she did.

Every year, the family would dig up plots of land for the students at the high school to supplement their food supply. They even had contests at the end of the season for the best gardens. She didn't participate in that. Because she was part faerie, she was one with the earth and had a huge advantage over all the others. But she still gardened here, and they had plenty of fresh things to eat, too.

Uncle Carroll and his mate Hanna would gather all the children around that were under twelve at the leap and have all-night movies and lots of food. It had been going on since before she'd been born, and it was sad when she'd become too old to join in. But that didn't mean that there wasn't anything for her to do when they were movie watching.

Uncle Leslie was a warlock and had the best Halloween parties. It was magical and fun. His mate, Aunt Veni, was teaching her some spells that she could use and even shared with her some of the magic that she had. It was wonderful having such a diverse family.

Then, there was her uncle Bailey. He was a hoot, and she loved him for all that he did for the family. Grannie Morgan would fuss at him for no reason just so that he'd tease her into a better mood. He was good at that. Having a good time.

The doctor in the family, even though they didn't really have a need for one, was her uncle Marley. He and Sin had headed up all kinds of projects for the little town that they lived in so that everyone would be healthier and happier. There were no homeless in town either, thanks fully to their efforts. Getting people healthy meant that they could work. And there was always a job in town that they could work at. She loved to see the faces of some of the people when they were able to get their first paycheck after being without for so long.

The phoenix population had grown, too, thanks to her aunt Allison and Uncle Scout. Not only were there a great many of them around now, but they were being seen across the globe too. No one seemed to understand where they'd been hiding all this time, but it mattered little. They were great creatures, and she loved holding them when they were just chicks finding their way in the world they'd been born to.

Her grandpa Shiloh had always been there for her. Like this week, he'd waited on her to tell him what she'd been feeling. He'd always been there for her. They were alike the two of them. A shifter leopard that had wings and could fly. She wasn't nearly as big as he was yet, but she knew that she could out-size any of the other children who grew up on this land.

He also told her that she'd find her mate someday, and they'd take over his job and that of Grandma Rocky in keeping the kingdom of Tellus safe. She knew that was a long way off. Grandda

Shiloh had been an ancient when he'd found his mate. And she knew that while it could be tomorrow or a thousand years from now, she'd treat him the same way that her family treated their mates, too, with dignity and respect. Or Grannie Morgan would bring a pain down on her head that would last several more lifetimes.

"What are you doing there, child?" She smiled at Thad, and he came closer to her to see what she was about. "Well, isn't that just about the prettiest picture that I've ever seen?"

"You said that yesterday when you saw my lilac painting, Uncle Thad." He told her that this one was much prettier. "Thank you. I thought that you and Sammy were headed out to see some other areas you'd been having trouble with."

"Oh, he went and solved the problem last evening. Just popped over there, rolled some heads, and then got them working at what they should have been doing all along. I tell you, having him taken over for me as the king of gnomes was the best move I've ever made." She told him that she thought he'd done a good job in training him as well. "Thank you, child. I do need to hear that on occasion."

One day, so long ago that no one remembered

the date anymore, Thad had been in the yard when some wild dogs had attacked the gnome. He'd nearly died and would have had it not been for her older cousin Sammy. While he was healing, Thad had noticed how much he'd been missing as king and had asked Sammy's parents if it would be all right with them if he took over his job. Of course, being the wonderful aunt and uncle they were, they had left that decision up to their son. She thought that Uncle Marley and Aunt Sin had the right idea in letting him decide. He was a wonderful king but a hard one when it came to making sure that the world was a much better place for them being there.

Making her way home after supper, she picked a few of the late blooms that wouldn't be as pretty tomorrow to give to her mom. She'd go on and on about them until she would regret it, but she loved her parents so much she knew that she'd put up with just about anything to see them smile at her.

Lying in bed that night, she got up to open her window. The faeries would come in soon, and they'd settle in her room like they always did. Once they were all inside, she lay looking up at her ceiling where they were and thought about how long they'd been around. Longer than even her grandparents and had seen more than any living creature around.

"You do know that you'll see much in the way of changes, too, my lady." She turned and smiled at Rand as he landed on her pillow. "You've so much to look forward to, and I'm excited to be there with you when it does."

"Don't tell me." He said that he'd not do that. "Thank you. I want my life to be full of surprises at every turn. I'm not saying don't tell me something I need to know. You know, like finding my mate. I don't want to hurt him or anything when he comes around just because I'm being silly or something."

"You'll not do that. You'll be as good and kind as the others have been—not to say they didn't get off on the wrong foot, a few of them, but they loved harder than even faeries do, and I think that we love the best." She handed him a flower from the few that she'd taken out of her mom's flowers. "Why, thank you. This is a good treat before bed. Would you mind if I shared a bit of it?"

"No. I brought in a lot so that everyone that wants some of them could have them." She laid the fading blooms on her pillow. "They won't be fit to eat tomorrow. So enjoy."

While they were still going through what they

wanted, Albry felt her eyes grow heavy. Tomorrow was going to be a good day, and she was going to wrap both hands around it and enjoy it to the limit. After all, she was a part of the Morgan Leap.

~*~

Morgan had wanted this to happen decades ago. However, the means to have it done weren't available back then, and when it was, she was simply too busy to get it organized. But now, more than ever, she needed this to work.

Her family was just too big to get all of them together, and she thought that if she could just get a picture of herself with her sons and daughters, she'd be content about a lot of things. Perhaps not content, but she'd be happy with this for a long time. She'd been feeling melancholy of late, and she hated that feeling. This was just what she needed. A little pick me up that would make her feel less sad and thrilled about how things were going. Frankly, she thought that she was just bored, but there was no way she was going to mention that to anyone. They'd have her cleaning out stalls or something.

They had told her that they'd be here at two this afternoon. It was nearly one-thirty now, and she'd not seen hide nor hair of any of the fourteen of them. Smiling to herself, she did realize that wrangling up fourteen people to sit with her was asking the impossible, but she knew that they could do it if anyone could. Having her six boys, three step-children—who she loved as much as her sons and her four daughters and son together was going to be a rare treat for her. They were all as busy as she'd been when she'd first taken over the care of Morgan's Leap all those years and years ago.

"Hey, Mom." Shiloh would be the first one here, and he didn't disappoint her. After she hugged and kissed him on the cheek he handed her his empty tin that held his own stash of cookies. "The others are outside waiting on us. I had to—I was glad to move things around. Having a crew working for me is making my life a good deal better. Did I tell you that I only need to work in the castle until noon, then I'm done for the day? Unless an emergency comes up. But even that doesn't take all that long to fix. How are you doing? Oh, and my tin is empty again. I just don't know who is eating all my stash."

"The others brought their tins over last night. My goodness, I guess I'll be baking again soon." He sat down on the barstool and smiled at her. "Everything all right? You seem sort of, I don't know, silly today."

"I feel silly, as a matter of fact. More giddy, I guess. When was the last time that we had everyone together like this? I think it's been at least a decade or two. I think the last time was when we had the first Earth Day. That was — wow, that was a bit ago." She said that she had missed the dinners they had together. "Me too. Especially with Tom and his kids and our sisters and brother. We need to get that going again. Even if we have to do it in a couple of nights."

"I'd like that." She heard something out front and started for the door. It was Carroll coming in the door, and she settled into the kitchen again with the two of them. "We were just talking about getting us all together. I was thinking about how large of a family we were just yesterday. I have fifty-one grandchildren. Do you believe it?"

"Mom, you would adopt every child in the town if they'd let you. I'm sure that most of the kids call you Grandma Morgan anyway." She smiled and said that they did. "Then you'd have to count the great-grandchildren and the great-great ones. Christ, I think you might well have over three thousand descendants around here. It's wonderful to know, too, that we have so much family. I know it makes me feel good."

"Not all of them are around anymore. I think it was a good idea to just let the first generation live on the land here, and the others, once they were ready to go out into the world, go their way in teaching the methods that we have here. I think it's made a huge difference in the world, too." They both agreed with her. "I can see them anytime I want, but getting us all together? I don't think that is going to ever happen again. Not unless we rented out a massive building or something. Can you imagine the food bill that we'd have? It would be fun, however, don't you think?"

"Yes." They both answered her at the same time. She looked at the clock. It was now about ten till two, and she was beginning to worry. It was Shiloh who took her hand into his before speaking. "They'll be here, Mom. Don't worry. We promised to make this work, and none of us want to disappoint you."

"I know that. But you're all so busy. The photographer said that if someone wasn't able to make it today, he could put them into the picture anyway. It will be what I want but not too. I want us all to be standing together." Shiloh assured her that they would be. "You're terribly sure of yourself. What do you know?"

"It's time." She looked at Scout when he came

in the back door. She asked him what he was talking about. "It's just time, that's all. Come on out. The photographer is here, and we can all get a picture together. I've already explained to him that we want copies made for each of us. And some to send out to our families, too. I think he's excited to be asked to do this for you. I hadn't realized that he was part of your pay-it-forward plan from several years ago. He's become quite famous, hasn't he?"

"I guess he has. But that was all on him. I only picked him up and shook him off a bit when he kept causing trouble at school. He was a good kid but just needed someone to believe in him. And we all did. He turned out all right, I think." She started for the front of the house. "I won't let this take up your whole day, boys, but I so want—"

The door opened, and she stepped outside onto the porch. As she turned to continue talking to her boys, she looked around. Putting her hand over her mouth, she could only stare at the sight that greeted her. They came.

They were all there. Not just her children, all of them, but their families too. And theirs beyond them and so on. She looked at all the faces staring at her, and she felt her eyes fill with tears. Her children, her family had come home to have their picture taken with her. And for the first time in longer than she could remember, Morgan was rendered speechless.

There were hundreds of people — adults and children — just waiting for her to come to see them. Children that she'd not seen yet. More mates that she'd not had the chance to meet. They were all waiting, and she couldn't hold back the tears any longer as they smiled at her.

Walking around them all, she couldn't believe that this was happening. She had to touch each of them, their faces or hands. She didn't care that her face was a mess. She'd just blame it on allergies, though she was sure no one would believe her.

Her family had done this for her, and she couldn't have been more pleased or happy. So many memories flooded her mind that she had a feeling that this was going to sustain her for the rest of her days. Promising that she'd visit each and every one of them when the picture was taken, it was Shiloh who stood next to her when she and Tom were positioned on the steps with their family behind them. Morgan couldn't help but continue to look behind her. They really were all here, and she wanted to make sure that they weren't a dream come true for her.

"Mom. We have one more surprise for you." She cried a bit more, telling him that she didn't know how much more she could take. After a quick hug, he smiled at her. "Oh, I think you'll love this one so much better. I want you to look just over there. At the barn."

At first, she couldn't see anything. Then, as her eyes adjusted to the shadow of trees, she saw a cat. A leopard. Then, the doorway of the big barn was filled with more of them. But it was the one that was limping and coming to her that caught her attention.

"Her name is Shi. She's the oldest living descendant of Golden Eyes that you saved the night of your parent's death. Shi made this trip because she wanted to meet you before she passed on. The others, they're her children that she says she'd not have if not for you and your love of their mother." Morgan didn't know how she had made it to where the big cat was, but she was suddenly in front of her. "She's been making her way here for days and only just arrived this morning."

Getting on her knees in front of the large cat, Morgan bowed her head so that her nose nearly touched the earth. When the hot breath blew over her neck, she put up her hand. Morgan could feel her hand trembling. She was both nervous and excited to meet Shi. When her hand was licked, Morgan sat up and hugged the great cat to her.

"You look so much like she did. Even your eyes are the same color." The two of them hugged the great paws of the other cat wrapped over her shoulders so that she felt her love. "Oh, how I wish I could talk to you."

Shiloh sat down on the ground next to her. "She'll be able to understand you perfectly fine. All the cats since Golden have the ability to understand humans. But I'll translate for her. She didn't think having a connection to you would be good. Shi told me that she is a wild cat and she'd rather not have you worrying about the way that she's living. Also, she said that she's not long for this earth but wanted more than anything to come to meet you. They all call you the mother of all cats." When the cat spoke through her son, it was as if she was speaking directly to her.

"When we were but small kittens, our parents would tell us the story of the great mother cat. How one night, she came to a cave full of leopards and saved three tiny kittens and their mother. Our mother." Morgan closed her eyes, remembering the night like it was just a few hours ago. "Generation after generation tells the same story, the same way, so that you will always be a part of our lives. The human child that not only took wild animals into her own home but raised the sons of our mother as her own. Making them a part of the world, a kinder part of the world as we know it."

"I would do it all again, too." Shi told her that they knew that as well. That her love was nothing like other humans had toward the wild, but special. "Yes, and my love for Golden was special, too."

"Yes, we talk about that love. And what you've done for us all." The cat turned to the group that was there with her, watching Morgan's family getting to know the cats like they were family. "These children of her children have been accompanying me since I was told of this day. I've come here to tell you that your love is far-reaching, your story even further told. Morgan, queen of the shifters, mother to the children of the first leopard shifters, we have come here this day to thank you for everything that you've done for us. In keeping us and all animals safe."

The sack was brought out of the barn by one of the younger cats. When it was set before her, Morgan told Shi that she had no need for gifts, that them being there was more than she could have hoped for in all her lifetimes. Then she opened the large sack and dumped the large stone on the ground.

"It's a cat's eye." The stone, beautifully polished, laid on the green grass and gleamed with the sun dancing over it. It must have weighed upwards of thirty pounds, and the eye looking center looked like it had been painted on the stone rather than done naturally. Running her hand over the smooth surface, all she could think about was how much it looked like the giver, the golden eyes of the first Golden. "I don't know what to say. It's beyond anything that I've ever seen before. I'll treasure it forever."

After talking to the cats for a while, the photographer asked if he could get the picture before the sun settled much more. Morgan had completely forgotten about the photo and was glad that the cats, all of them, were going to join in the photo, too. As soon as they were all set, Shi sitting on the steps that she and Tom were on, the much-anticipated picture took no time at all to be captured.

Morgan thought of herself as one of the luckiest people on earth. Not only did she have a grand family, but that family extended far beyond anything that she'd ever had thought of before. The children of Golden, from all those years and years ago, had come to see her, and Morgan thought that if she were to be able to die right now, she'd do so with so much happiness in her heart that she'd be content to move on. There would be no unfinished details of her life left behind.

The picture, along with the stone, was going to be over her fireplace. Morgan realized while sitting in the sun with her family that it held a lot of treasures from her life. Teeth of the boys when they'd been kittens. Other things that she'd found in the woods while taking a walk. Things that the grandchildren had made. Trinkets they would get for her when they were just hanging out together. There were pictures, too. Photographs of the kids in school. On outings, too. She would need to take it all down now and store it away for new memories, like the one from today.

"You're the best mother that could have ever been chosen for us." She hugged Shiloh and the others when they joined her under the shade tree. "We wanted to tell you how much we loved you, and I think that this was the best possible way."

"Yes. It was." She laid her head back, feeling better than she thought she had in years. "I love you guys. Each and every one of you. And I can't thank you enough for today. Only in telling you how much I love it. And you."

That night, while the house was sleeping, Morgan sat in the living room and watched the stars twinkle. She had a perfect view of the night sky, and she had spent many a nights in this same position, just waiting for the sun to come up. And after today, that very thing would mean so much more to her because of her family. Morgan was happier now than she'd been in a long time, and it was because of a simple request that turned into a wonderful day. Life couldn't be any better than it was right now for her.

Before You Go...

HELP AN AUTHOR

write a review

THANK YOU!

Share your voice and help guide other readers to these wonderful books. Even if it's only a line or two, your reviews help readers discover the author's books so they can continue creating stories that you'll love. Log in to your favorite retailer and leave a review. Thank you.

AWARD WINNING, BESTSELLING AUTHOR

Kathi Barton, a winner of the Pinnacle Book Achievement Award and a best-selling author on Amazon and All Romance books, lives in Nashport, Ohio, with her husband, Paul. When not creating new worlds and romance, Kathi and her husband enjoy camping and going to auctions. She can also be seen at county fairs with her husband, an artist and potter.

Her muse, a cross between Jimmy Stewart and Hugh Jackman, brings her stories to life for her readers in a way that has them returning for more. Her favorite genre is paranormal romance, with a great deal of spice. You can visit Kathi online and email her if you'd like. She loves hearing from her fans. aaronskiss@gmail.com.

www.ingramcontent.com/pod-product-compliance
Lightning Source LLC
Chambersburg PA
CBHW030226180626
46810CB00008B/2999